# Alone not lonely

Also by Maureen Mendelowitz and published by Ginninderra Press
*The Rock*

Maureen Mendelowitz

# Alone not lonely

*Alone not lonely*
ISBN 978 1 76041 613 3
Copyright © text Maureen Mendelowitz 2018
Cover design by Robyn Zeller
Cover image: Taryn Tollman, *Art in Glass*

First published 2018 by
GINNINDERRA PRESS
PO Box 3461 Port Adelaide 5015
www.ginninderrapress.com.au

From Julian –

…and we shall make of our lives a bouquet…


For Julian –

Always…

She found the packet on a Thursday. Floating in an oily pool of water. At the bus stop.

The day had broken red, indicating rain. A bank of clouds flamed on the skyline. The trees were quiet. All was quiet except for the distant call of a lonely bird.

In the yard, the heat built. The air hardly moved. It piled, layer upon layer. Each year, the plums grew in abundance, ripened to purple and burst from their skins with honey-sweet indigo juice. They were like hothouse plums, nurtured in a constant environment.

The dog pushed onto four legs, stretched forward then back and stretched its jaws. It sniffed at the bowl of water, where tiny insects floated, rejected the water and stretched again. It turned round a couple of times, unsure, contemplating what to do next.

A door in a passageway under the garages opened. At once, the dog was attentive, cocking its ears. It bounded towards a woman bunched in a dressing gown, licking the backs of her exposed ankles in slippers with the backs bent inwards.

'*Haai* Blackie!' she muttered, then swore at the plums that had splattered on the path. Armies of ants commandeered the bursts of voluptuous fruit, devouring the flesh and sticking in the oozing blue juices. '*Fok!*' she said with resentment.

But being who she was, she would clean the mess. Because cleaning was who she was. It was her job. But it was also her talent, her pastime, her hobby. It was the one thing that saved her from when she was a child. Wiping, rubbing, sweeping, scrubbing allowed her to lose herself. To be in her own world. To be divorced from what she did not want to know. The harder she rubbed, the less she saw or felt. Cleanliness became the thing that sustained her.

Standing solidly in the bath, she lathered soap under her arms and breasts, around her stomach, between her legs and in the crease of her square backside. She brushed her neck and back and feet, meticulously removing every smell that may have settled on her during the night. She brushed her teeth then brushed her hair into a tight bun, holding hairpins between her teeth.

She buttoned herself into a pink overall, tied the matching apron around her waist, slipped her feet into worn brown sandals and stepped into the kitchen.

Jarryd was looking for a soccer sock. He said there was only one in the drawer.

'There was two,' Minnie told him.

'There's only one,' he shouted.

'I'm coming,' she said, putting coffee grains in the percolator. She sliced melon for Mark, put the cereals out, the milk, the yoghurt and the bananas. She boiled the kettle for Dana's tea.

'Minnie!' Jarryd yelled.

'I'm coming.' She made and packed the sandwiches – peanut butter and honey, cheese and jam – and the muesli bars and apples, and a banana for Jeremy.

In Jarryd's room, the sock drawer had been pulled out and emptied onto the floor. 'There's only one! I've got to have the right socks otherwise I can't play!'

She searched through the socks, got onto her knees, peered into the drawer cavity and found the other sock stuck at the back. She packed the socks, put the drawer back and clambered heavily onto her feet.

'Minnie,' called Dana, 'when my tea's ready, you can bring it. I'm up.'

'Yes, *Merrem*.' She went down the carpeted stairs, the stairs that she brushed each day.

Mark was in the kitchen. He munched the cereal, his tie undone, his top button undone, his jacket slung on the back of a chair. 'Morning,' he mumbled through the masticated food without looking up. 'Tell the boys to hurry up. I've got to leave. If any of them keep me waiting this morning, they can find their own way.'

'Yes, *Mastah*.'

She laid the tea tray with bone china, the teapot, the milk jug, the dainty cup and saucer. Dana liked plain and elegant. But good. It had to be good. She used bone china every day.

'Jeremy. Jarryd. Your daddy says you mus' be quick. You still mus' eat. You mus' *mos* make quick now. He say he won't wait.'

She balanced the tray on one hand and knocked on the door of Dana's bedroom with the other. The room was filled with mellow light filtering through sheer voile curtains. The damasks were drawn back, but the windows had not been opened and the air was stale with sleep and Dana's perfume. The bed was a tumble of pillows and sheets and blankets. Mark's underpants and socks lay on the floor and yesterday's suit was crumpled on the blue silk chair.

Dana was curled on the chaise longue, her negligée open, her long thin legs exposed, her ear to the phone. 'That is unbelievable!' she was saying. 'Honestly. I cannot believe what you're telling me! She's something else, that woman…' She motioned for the tea tray to be set beside her.

Jarryd and Jeremy burst into the room, brushing past Minnie. They presented rosy faces for kisses. Dana smoothed the cockscomb that stood at the back of Jarryd's head, kissed their sweet cheeks without interrupting her conversation and blew them kisses.

'Hey, boys!' Mark's voice came yelling from the hall. 'If you don't come now, you can walk.' They dashed from the room, their shirts not properly in their short pants, their socks not properly pulled up.

Minnie picked up the washing and the wet towel on the floor in the bathroom.

'Oh God! Just a mo', Mari. Minnie, quickly! Bring me my bag.' She found her purse, carefully hooking out some coins with manicured nails. 'Quickly. Give this to the boys. Tuckshop money,' she laughed into the phone. 'Mark's never got any change on him. Go! Quickly!' she motioned. 'Catch them before they leave.'

Minnie lumbered down the stairs with the coins, cursing. She shared the money between the boys, who were munching their cereal and sliced bananas. Jarryd had spilt sugar on the table and was drawing in it. She put their lunches in their bags then went back up the stairs to collect the washing.

Jeremy had wet his bed again. The room stank of urine.

Every day was the same hurrying and scurrying, the losing and finding, the scrambling, the panic. The maid tried to organise the boys, to have their uniforms ready, their breakfasts in place, their lunches packed. But there was always some reason for her to climb the stairs, to rush down again. 'If the *Merrem* see to them, it would be better. But she's always lying in the bed.'

Minnie moved around the house with her duster and *lappies*, opened the windows and threw out a bowl of drooping flowers.

She made the beds and mopped the bathroom floors and wiped the kitchen table and swept the sugar from the floor.

She gave the dog biscuits and fresh water.

She hung the washing on the revolving lines.

Blackie always barked at the washing. She wondered whether the dog saw the master's wet shirts inflated by wind as intruders. She wondered about Blackie. Does it have brains? It eats when it feels hungry. It drinks. It sleeps. It barks when it's frightened. It wags its tail and jumps around when it sees the children. But can it think? She did not think so. 'It jus' goes along with its instinc'.'

But then, when she sits in her room, slumped at her table, her feet swollen and bare, and stares at the floor, the dog pats in quietly and lays a paw on her foot and timidly looks up at her from lidded eyes.

Then she thinks maybe it can think…

A white light poured into the yard. The south-easter was howling, whipping the washing and causing plums to crash. She heard ominous rumbles in the distance.

A blinding flash of lightning and a terrible blast of thunder made Blackie yelp and scratch frantically at the back door. Huge splotches of rain splashed hard against the kitchen windows.

'*Fok*.' She grabbed the laundry basket and ran out. With thick nimble fingers, she unpegged and roughly pulled the washing from the wildly revolving line. There were blobs of rain on the clothes, but those she could iron dry. Hugging the basket in both arms, she thumped back to the kitchen, a corner of a sheet dragging behind her in the mud.

The dog was mad around her ankles.

The clouds, a dark ominous grey blanketing the skies, were viciously pierced by stabs of blinding lightning. Rain fell in seamless torrents. Through the windowpanes, the trees were wavy, as though under water. The mountain, a rugged and impressive background to the house, was now a brown and running smudge.

This was the kind of storm that one shrank from, drew curtains on, blocked out by covering one's ears. It would cease as quickly as it had started, leaving the gardens drenched, flower heads broken, trees glittering like chandeliers, the gutters strongly flowing.

The next day, there would be flashes on the mountainside, perpendicular needles of waterfalls brilliantly captured by the rays of the sun.

It was her afternoon off, her time to go to the OK Bazaars to buy sweets for her nephews and a fruit cake for her sister-in-law. She could see them in her mind's eye, the two boys swinging on a creaking blue gate. They would run to her, dance around her, exclaim in their reedy sing-song voices, '*Daar's* Auntie! Hello, Auntie!' – watching her with rounded eyes, grinning with gaps in their teeth and dried snot around their nostrils. Two bony boys with scabs on their knees.

She wore her coat and her closed shoes down the hill to the bus shelter. Sun was filtering through pale wisps of disappearing cloud. The gutters overflowed, swift-flowing streams taking leaves and a sodden newspaper. The trees glistened greenly. The road gleamed. A clean smell of after-rain hung in the air.

She took a chance. Sat on the WHITES ONLY bench. Leaned forward to ensure that her feet were out of an oily puddle and saw the envelope, a thick brown envelope with PAY PACKET stamped in big letters across it. She picked it up by one sodden corner. 'Someone mus've drop it. They'll come an' look for it.'

The seal had come away. She lifted the fold. Inside was a wad of notes. Money. A lot of money.

'*Ghott!*' she gasped. Frightened, she dropped the envelope next to her foot. Without knowing why, she felt guilty, as though she had been accused. She looked away and stared at nothing, telling herself, 'Someone lose this. They will come back to find it.' She gave it another furtive glance then stared at her fingers that were twisting together.

A man crossed the road. He wasn't in a rush. He didn't seem upset. He didn't look as though he'd lost anything. He walked across the road towards the bus stop like any person would.

All these thoughts flashed through Minnie's mind. What would he do if he saw the envelope?

He would pick it up. Jus' *sommer so*. Without it belonging to him.

He wouldn't ask if it was hers. He would just take it. Put it in his pocket.

An' what about her? She saw it first. What would she do? She couldn't ask for it back. It didn't belong to her.

So he would get the money. And she would get nothing.

'No!' her mind said and in a flash her broad foot covered the envelope.

They waited for the bus. Minnie's face was a mask. Her eyes were like stones.

If no other person came along to claim that money, she would take it. She found it. She never stole it. 'What they say – finders keepers losers weepers…'

Beads of sweat appeared on her upper lip.

Where was the bus?

When it came, the man stood up. She stared ahead, waiting for him to board. Then, as quick as a wink, she pocketed the envelope and found her way to an allocated seat at the back of the bus.

Turning her face to the window, she stared unseeingly at raindrops clinging to the pane, blowing into rivulets that ran down the smudged glass.

Her hand slipped surreptitiously into her pocket. She felt the package. Her fingers closed around it.

The bus trundled down the hill, stopping and starting. Mist covered the windows. Minnie sat without moving, not hearing or seeing, until she heard the driver call, 'Terminus. All out. *Almal uit.*'

Her mind had become numb and numbness crept up her legs. The crease between her breasts was damp.

She remained seated. She knew that she could not do her usual shop today. Not with that envelope in her pocket.

A white light pushed through the smeared windows. The air was thick. Minnie's heart exploded in her chest. Her hands trembled. Her mouth was dry. She felt ill. She urgently needed to get back to her room.

After what seemed like an age, the bus trundled back up the hill.

Steam smoked from the road as she clambered off at her bus stop and walked woodenly up the back path of the house and into the yard.

Blackie, curled into an afternoon sleep, heard her through the gate. Mad with excitement, the dog rushed towards her yelping, then cavorted around the yard crazily chasing its tail.

The neighbours told Dana they did not know how to look after a dog. Poor animal. Locked up in the yard like that. All day. No one to walk it. No one to take any notice of it. That's why it barks like that. They shouldn't have a dog. That's what they told Minnie over the wall one day. Madam tossed her head and said that Blackie was a watchdog. To keep all the visitors away. She didn't want rubbish *skollies* in the yard. To hell with the neighbours, she'd said. The dog was none of their bladdy business. To hell with them! They'll just have to live with it.

'Git away, Blackie. *Haai!* Git away!'

She pushed the dog from her door and locked it behind her. Leaning against it with all her weight, she felt for the envelope. Her legs were as heavy as lead. Her face was beaded with sweat.

She moved towards the table, sank heavily into a chair and stared at the envelope. Lifting the flap, she gasped at the thick wad of notes. With stiff fingers, she removed it from the sodden cover and stared, not breathing, her body trembling and her heart beating hard and fast.

She wondered how much there was. She mus' count it. With a tightly clenched fist, she held down the notes then licked her forefinger and slowly, deliberately, began to flick the corners.

'*Ghott!*' she exclaimed. Leaning back, she shook her head, disbelieving.

Then hunching her thick shoulders, and with spit from her bottom lip on her finger she counted again. She leaned back again, sat immobile, then counted for a third time.

'*Ghott!*'

Hastily, clumsily, she shoved the pile back into the envelope in a frantic attempt to hide it from imaginary eyes that were greedily watching it. From imaginary hands that wanted to grab it.

The room began to close in on her. The locked door, the tightly shut window, the drawn curtains, the insipid light. The raincoat that she still wore. Her closed shoes.

A grey film stuck to her face. Her body was clammy and her armpits smelled of sweat. She was finding difficulty in expelling the air from her lungs. With thumping heart and rapid breath she stood up holding the edge of the table, then walked unsteadily to the window and opened it a little.

She told herself that she had to work fast. She had to find a hiding place. Somewhere that no one would find. But where?

With the envelope back in her pocket, she examined the room with her eyes. Up to the picture rail. A picture hung there of the sea. Behind the picture? If she hung it higher, the envelope could rest on the rail and be hidden by the sea. But no. That wouldn't work. Every time she needed to get to it, she'd have to stand on a chair.

There was the little cupboard with the mugs and the tea. What about under the box of tea? No. Anyone can find that. Same with under the packet of biscuits…

There was under the mattress, under the bed, in the suitcase.

There was under her pillow.

In her wardrobe.

Under a shoebox.

Inside a shoe.

Inside the pocket of her Sunday dress.

There was under the little rug.

Sweat dripped between her breasts. She wiped her face with a handkerchief and sank back into the chair, her hands clutching the ends of the table.

She moved her hands under the table. Her thick fingers were anxiously exploring. She felt something. A little space. Clumsily, heavily, she went down on her knees, turning her face upwards under the table. There was a small ledge where the top was joined to the legs. It was narrow but it was a space. A space to hide the money. If she rolled it up tightly, she could get it in there.

She was instantly alert. With nimble fingers, she wrapped the notes into a fat cigar. She tried the space. No. Too small. She undid the little parcel and rolled the notes lengthwise and very tight. This time it fitted. A tight squeeze, but it was in and wouldn't budge without her dislodging it.

She bent down and examined the hiding place with her upside-down face and her big fingers. She stood up and studied the table. She walked around the table and stared at it from every angle.

It needed to be covered.

'*Yirrah!* It mus' be covered.'

Down on her knees again, she grunted as she hauled the suitcase from under the bed and pulled out a tablecloth that she was keeping for something special. Without sentiment, without her natural reverence for new things, she shook out the cloth and draped it over the table. There was plenty of drop on all sides. She pulled at it. This way and that until she was satisfied.

Minnie stood squat. She looked down at the cloth.

Her hands pressed down hard onto the red and yellow flowers that flared through the gloom.

Her heart pounded.

She shut her eyes tight as though in prayer.

Then, with all her strength, with all her might, she willed that, 'Please. Please. Please. This table mus' keep my secret safe.'

A pale light pushed against the closed window, through the gap in the drawn curtain. The air was dank and close. A damp corner smelled of mould.

Minnie, on her back, her mouth open, snored loudly, her hands clasped over her breasts. Throughout the night, she'd padded over to the table and felt for the parcel.

No sooner had she dozed off than she woke. She thought that someone was in the room, that someone was lifting that corner of the tablecloth, and she would clap her hands together or bang one hand on her heart and say aloud, 'My *Ghott!*'

She checked the door to see that it was locked. She checked the window. She clambered back into bed shivering. She put on her gown then took it off. The *doekie* she wound around her head to protect her pillowcase from loose hairs was entangled in the bedclothes.

She sipped water.

Late into the night, she found herself rocking to and fro to alleviate the agitation that overcame her. Then, in the hours when a pale light struggled to enter, she placed the parcel between her breasts and fell asleep.

She'd gone compulsively past the bus shelter looking for someone who was looking for the money. Out of the corner of her eye, she saw a man sitting reading his newspaper. A schoolboy squatted on his suitcase chewing gum. She thought, 'It's not the man. He's not looking. Can't be the boy. How can he get so much money?'

She'd turned at the corner and sauntered back slowly, seemingly unconcerned, but with her heart beating fast and her nails biting into palms. A woman was now sitting there and she was looking around, at the ground, at the road, at the pavement, and back at the ground. As Minnie passed, they exchanged glances.

'My *Ghott!* She panicked. 'Maybe it's her. Maybe she's the one. I wunner if she's the one? I wunner if it's her? She looks like she looking!'

Compelling herself not to rush, and willing herself not to look back, she said aloud, '*Yirrah!* Why am I here? It's late. I mus' get back! I mus' do the ironing! *Ghotts!* I mus' go make the supper!'

She fixed her gaze firmly on the pavement, quickened her step and tried to swallow her agitation. '*Haai* man!' Minnie scolded herself, 'you find this money! You find it. Your keep it. You never take it. You find it. You never steal it. You find it. It belong to you. If I leave it someone else took it. *Haai* man! I mus' go back! I mus' do the ironing! I mus' make the supper!'

'God knows what's got into her!' Dana examined her nails. 'She jumps! I'm telling you. She literally jumps when you speak to her.' Dana laughed. 'Honestly, I walked into the kitchen just now to tell her something and she literally jumped out of her skin! What? No. She's usually quite *doff.* You know: Yes Madam No Madam. Like a block of wood. You don't know what's going on in her head. Very little sign of life. Mark says robotic. He calls her an automaton.

'But this is something new. She's really jumpy. God, I hope she doesn't *putt* out on me. The last thing I need in my life right now is to look for a new maid…

'Four years. Nearly four years. I think she started in February. Yes. It's almost four years. Oh look, she's OK. The main thing is, she doesn't have anyone coming here. Thank God for that! With the last one, there were people coming and going day and night. That's why Mark got the dog. That's another story. Remind me to tell you what went on with the neighbour and Mark last week about the bladdy dog…

'Oh well. I hope she gets over whatever's got into her. Who knows what goes on in their lives, and quite honestly I'm not really interested. As long as it doesn't impact on us. That's all I care about.'

For Minnie, Sunday was going to prove to be most difficult.

At work, she could check on her treasure or bring it with her into the house. She would put it in the sideboard drawer as she polished the table, or hide it under a cushion in the lounge when dusting, or keep it behind a box of soap powder when she ironed. She felt most comfortable having it near her and would have kept it between her breasts but it kept slipping, falling out.

Sunday was Minnie's day off. She always took a bus to Bonteheuvel. She would attend the service at the Coloured church she had gone to since she was a child. Then she would visit her nephew and his wife and, by five o'clock, be slowly climbing the hill, the wide tree-lined avenues, back to her room.

This was her routine for Sundays. Put on her freshly washed Sunday dress, her string of beads, her closed shoes, take the parcel of sweets and cake and walk down to the main road to catch the bus, all in a steady and sedate state of mind.

This Sunday caused her much turmoil.

She knew one thing. She knew she could not take the money with her. *Vragtig!* Not to Bonteheuvel. *Nee man!*

So the money had to stay in her room in the hiding place.

For the first time since she found it, she would be separated from it. The prospect of separation she was experiencing was an agony for her. Tormented, she spent much of the previous night convincing herself that the money would be safe. No one would break in. No one knew it was there. No one knew her secret. No one knew her hiding place.

It will be safe.

Better to stay here.

I can never take it with me to Bonteheuvel.

*Daardie diewe sal rook dit uit.* Those thieves will smell it out.

*Ny man! Dit moet hier bly. Dit sal* OK *wees.* It must stay here. It will be safe here.

*Seker…* For sure…

She chose to sit at the back of the church. From there, unnoticed in the smudged sunlight, she looked at the backs of people's heads and their necks, and the slopes of their shoulders.

Immediately in front of her was a woman who'd used straightener on her lifeless hair. A small girl perched on her knees on the seat had tightly braided plaits like knotted string tied with blue ribbons, perhaps also, in effort to remedy *kril* hair. She remembered the agonising pull on her own telltale hair all those years ago, and the terrible scratch from a starched collar, and long white socks that crumpled and shoe leather coated and cracked with Shu-Shine white shoe paint.

Dust motes danced on shafts of light that pushed through the smeared windowpanes and shunted into the gloom. The soft glow seemed, she thought, as though sent by God himself. She breathed in the comfort, the sense of people sitting quietly together, present and dignified.

There was no smell of liquor, no bottled frustrations, no anger or fear in this quietude.

The women absorbed the protection offered by this humble building and were filled with serenity and peace.

The minister's words flowed through them, sonorous and clear despite a cough, the clearing of a throat, a shuffle of shoes on the wooden floor.

Was it the right thing to lose your identity by trying for white?

Was it right to turn your back on your own people by pretending you were white?

What about the indignity of the testing? The lack of respect, the gross insult of having your fingernails examined to see if the half moons were mauve?

Or having a pencil inserted in your hair to see if it stuck in the kinks, then you were coloured.

Or fell out – then you were white?

She thought of her sister, whom they no longer saw, of the German she married, of her straight hair and olive skin. She still thought of her as coloured, a coloured trying to live a white woman's life.

The sweet sound of the choir rose in praise of the Lord, the congregation shifted and rustled the pages of their hymn books and joined in.

Psalms swelled and filled the corners of the church, reaching into the ceiling, as in one voice the people sang, rejoicing in Jesus, Son of God.

The sun was hot on the dusty potholed street as Minnie walked to her nephew's house.

A small boy in torn trackies muttering, 'Sorry, Auntie,' bowled a flat bicycle wheel past her. It swerved and bounced along the broken pavement, somehow managing to stay upright.

As always, she averted her eyes from the facade of a cracked building, from the huge drawing of red parted lips, painted sideways, with the words *JOU MA SE POES* in red letters above it.

The shop entrance next to the artwork belched a smell of fried *snoek* and stock fish and a rancid smell of cooking oil.

A man on the corner was selling watermelons from a cart. She passed a split melon, succulent and red, oozing juice.

*Ook soos Ma se poes.* Like your mother's vagina…

Through the gate swinging on one hinge and up the broken path, the yard full of weeds surrounded by a sagging fence, to the blue front door of the blue house, the house that Devin had painted when they moved in. A blue house with *lekker* white windowsills. He'd even planted things. Wanted to make the place nice.

Minnie could not work out what went wrong with Devin. He used to be a nice boy, married to a nice girl, a girl whose mother served in a shop and dressed nice. She was a good girl, a good mother to their two boys, 'kept them clean and dressed so nice'. For a few years, they were respectable in a newly painted blue house and a neat yard and two good little boys. Then without warning Devin started to drink. Like his father. Like his father's brothers. Like Minnie's father. Like all the men in their family.

Four brothers. Two dead. One from a stroke, the other *moord*, knifed in a dark lane. The murderer was never caught. They kept going to Wynberg Police Station to find out, 'What is happening?' but the sergeant always gave them the same answer – no news. '*Ons soek*, but we haven't got him yet.'

Until they lost interest and stopped going.

But Sue-Ellen, who, as a teenager, changed her name from Ellen and took on the name of a beautiful woman in a daily soap opera, kept the house neat. She cut and glued new linoleum onto the kitchen floor, sewed curtains for the windows, scrubbed and polished, washed and ironed and lost herself in keeping things clean at home and in her char jobs. She worked until, at night, she dropped off to sleep without dreaming, without any thought of the next day.

Unless Devin wanted her. Unless he ruthlessly used her. Unless he bruised her mouth and her nipples so that they painfully swelled and left her in anguish for days.

'Hello, Tannie! Carl! Ramon! Kom! Tannie Minnie is *hier*!' The children scrabbled around her with dark round eyes fixed onto her bag, trying to swing on the straps. '*Haai kinner*s. Wait! Tante Minnie will give you. *Kom*. Take your sweets. Give a kiss *vir* Tante Minnie! *Se dankie* and *gee vir haar 'n soen.*'

'*Dankie,* Min. *Kom. Kom binne. Ons sal tee drink.*'

Minnie had resolved on the bus ride to Bonteheuvel that she'd tell no one of her find. She knew that Sue-Ellen would sense something, would say, 'What is it, Auntie? What's wrong? You don't look right.'

She would not divulge the cause of the dark patches under her eyes, and the redness of her eyes. She would not talk of her wakefulness through the long nights and of the unrelenting unease that twisted inside her. In her mind, she checked again that she'd locked the door of her room, that the rolled package was safely tucked into the groove in the table, that the red and yellow flowers were camouflaging it, keeping it safe.

'*Nee wat.* I feel a bit tired, you know. The end of the year. *Ek is net 'n bietjie moeg.*' She shrugged dismissively.

'An' how's it going with you, Susie?' Minnie's eyes flicked across the young woman's bony shoulders, her thin arms, the protruding chest bones that rose and fell with each breath she took, the tiny wrists and overgrown square hands.

Reflected in Sue-Ellen's cushioned dark eyes was pain and wariness, but through her compressed lips she answered, '*Nee. Goed donkie.* Jus' very busy. *Ek het* twee extra jobs now by your *Merrem*'s mother and also by the mother-in-law. *Haai* Carl. Don't make so much noise! *Pa slaap.*' She glanced at a shut door. Distracted, she murmured, 'Tuesday to the mother. Thursday to the mother-in-law… Devin sleeps,' she whispered to Minnie and Clemmie Beyers, who shifted her huge bulk and slid her gaze from one to the other. 'You heard, Auntie Clemmie. *Jy'd gehoer hoe hy was las*' night… *Yirrah!* It was bad…'

Clementine had heard. Squatted behind the wall of her bedroom, her ear to the open pane, hidden by a thick curtain and peering through a small gap, she'd listened with horror and fascination to Devin, rolling drunk Devin, who'd shouted and banged things around, who'd pushed and shoved his wife from the kitchen to the bedroom and back to the kitchen, who had sworn every defamity and thrown a bottle onto the paving, where it smashed into a thousand glittering pieces in the yard, where the boys ran barefoot, who'd ranted and raved, and then, at one terrifying moment, had seemed to stare directly at Clemmie as if he knew she was there, daring her to appear, and she, petrified, had shrunk back in terror and taken herself in her voluminous nightie back to bed where, frightened, she'd covered her head to shut out the whole of the house next door.

'*Nee wat.*' It was safer to play dumb. 'I didn' hear anything! Was fas' asleep…' But she shook her head slowly from side to side. 'Jus' like his father,' she mouthed sidewise to Minnie, her tongue bulging in bubbles of flesh between the gaps in her teeth.

Minnie replied, 'Jus' like him an' jus' like my husband.'

She left without seeing her nephew, walked away from the ominous stultification of that Sunday afternoon, the brooding of that house following her along the uneven pavements, filling her mind with her own past as she sat on the bus staring, unseeing but remembering.

'*Ag wat. Dis mos* behind me. Over. Gone. *Ghott in Hemel.* Dankie. He's far from my life. Forever away. I will never take another man in my life. Never.' Her thick fingers clutched at her bag.

Claremont came into view. She got off at the cinema on the corner and walked slowly up the hill passing white walls overhung with long crimson strands of bougainvillea and clusters of golden bougainvillea. The air was perfumed with frangipani and honeysuckle and miniature oaks dressed in new green made moving patterns on the pavements.

As she climbed the hill, her own feelings of heaviness began to subside. She thought of her treasure, of her room, her small dark room where the sunlight was no longer allowed in.

She felt for the rolled money, took it out, stroked it with her thumb and replaced it.

Kicking off her shoes, she took off her Sunday dress, lay on her bed and closed her eyes against the world she'd known. The world she'd come from.

The blank Cape Flats
Apartheid's dump
The sand and wind
And all the laws
to find a way
To force the move

of Coloured folk
from urban street
to low-cost house
In shanty town
In shades of grey
In shades of brown

For Coloured folk
Who've lost their way
The in betweens
the go betweens
The dislocated
          people

who try who try
to identify
to make their way
without a say
Not black, not white
Now out of sight
The dislocated
          people

With wine and dope
A way to cope
With knives and blades
As all hope fades

Not black not white
Now out of sight
The dislocated
        people

Minnie was born into it. The Cape Flats. Harsh. Flat. Ugly. A place where the south-easter hurled sand from False Bay. Sand that got into everything. A place where clumps of thorny shrubs and small scrubby trees were brought to their knees, their heads shaved by sharp winds, huddling in the grey soil between the shifting dunes.

She was one of a large hard-bitten community who were removed from their homes in the city, from the Whites Only areas, and resettled in this desolate wind-torn place.

Christened Minetta (her mother liked exotic names), she soon became Minnie – a name that suited her better. The younger of two sisters, she'd inherited the dark skin, wide nose and *kroes* hair of a native ancestor. It was said of her that she was 'a throwback from a *kaffir*'.

But to herself she would sometimes think of the name Minetta. 'So *pragtig*,' she'd whisper. Her pretty name would remain the only pretty thing about her.

Her sister, on the other hand, refused to answer to any other name than Veronica. Vere, or Ron, or Ronnie would get no response from her. With her smooth olive skin and dancing eyes, she'd giggle and say, 'My *naam* is Veronica.' Veronica, seductive from a child, would cunningly roll her little body around, wriggle and squirm on her father's lap, pleasing him until his eyes filled with ecstasy. In these cunning ways, she knew that she would get *tiekies* and sixpences, ice cream, new shoes and, always, the red luscious middle of the watermelon.

The role Minnie played was to help her mother. From as far back as she could remember, she'd take the dirty dishes to the sink, stand on a box that was there for her, roll up her sleeves, fill the basin with hot soapy water and, with her little girl hands, clean the grease from the plates and pots. She took pride in the glow and shine of the washed crockery and beamed at her mother's praises for her efforts.

She also took dusters and wiped all the surfaces in the house, swept the outside path, and on her child knees sometimes scrubbed the floors. When the neighbours commented, her mother, lying on the couch smoking a cigarette, would say, '*Ny wat! Sy wit dit doen. Sy hou om alles skoon to maak.*' Her mother said that she liked to do it, liked to make everything clean. '*Dit lyk mooi*, Minnie,' she would say. '*Baie mooi. Jy's 'n goeie meidjie.* A good little maid.'

The child was fulfilled. An accepted part of the household. Cleaning became her comfort and her escape. As she rubbed and scrubbed, she would hum little tunes to herself. It was her way of side-stepping the uncontrollability that spilled out daily. That overflowed into the dark and ominous nights.

The nightmare comes. She's unable to move, pressed down by a suffocating weight, her face covered. In her sleep, Minnie turns her head from side to side, gasping for air. The pressure upon her becomes greater. Now she can't move her head. There are harsh thrusts against her body and she hold back cries of pain. She fights to breathe, tries to push against the weight, endeavours to move away from the hurt but is powerless, and she begins to fall into a black and sticky space. She wants to move her legs but they are like lead. The dark and wet suck her down and she slips into suffocating nothingness.

The nightmare comes without warning. Relentless and unchanging. It's tortured her since she was a child. It lurks in the depths of her darkness.

Minnie, the younger of two daughters, was a small thin child who cowered behind her mother and hid her shy smile behind her hands and kept her eyes down when spoken to and always stood with her legs crossed. It was as if she knew what she'd been born into, what her fate was.

Her time came to experience what her older sister endured, what her mother knew but chose to ignore. Her father waited until she was seven before he took her onto his lap. At first she was overwhelmed at his show of filial affection, having never experienced any kindness or warmth from him, only hard slaps or shouts from his liquor-ridden mouth. She did not understand the hardening of his penis and disliked the way he rubbed against her. She hated his exploring fingers and his unshaven stubble against her neck. All the while, her mother sat and knitted and stared at the television while her older sister slipped quietly out of the room. Her thin undeveloped body was the focus of her father's attention and she became his favourite. It was to her bed that he came at night, to lie on her and wet her pyjamas while she tried to turn her head from side to side to breathe but never to cry out, for she know instinctively not to do so.

She became even more withdrawn, would not speak to her sister or the children at school. She only nodded or shook her head when her mother spoke to her. Of the two girls, Minnie was the more intelligent, but her schoolwork suffered to such an extent that she was labelled stupid, a child who did not listen, who could hardly comprehend.

'*Daar's iets makeer met daardie kind,*' her teacher told the headmaster. 'Something very wrong with her.' He made a note to talk to Minnie's mother but that never happened.

Then, without warning, her father lost interest in her. He no longer came to her at night, never spoke to her, treated her like the shadow she'd become. She wondered whether it was because her monthly bleeding had begun. She accepted the release from her huge burden as a matter of fact. It had been and now it was gone. But her schoolwork did not improve and she continued to skulk around the corners of the building and sit on her own at break times. At home, her withdrawal from her family was largely ignored. Her sister, sulky and surly, was, as she'd always been, dismissive and uninterested.

Hiding behind the kitchen door, she heard the neighbour say, '*Daardie Minnie, sy's so stil. Net soos a dood persoon…* As quiet as a dead person…'

She remembers hearing sounds of groaning, and her mother protesting, and their bed creaking, and the sound of a hard slap like a bullet going off, and her mother sobbing in the bathroom. She made herself small by hugging into a tight ball and pulling the blanket over her head, and covered her ears with her hands.

She remembers her sister fighting with her father, trying to pull him off her mother, and being given a hard kick by him that left her gasping and crawling into Minnie's bed, hands over her mouth to stifle her sobs.

Through closed eyes, she recalled her father come into their room at night to lie with her sister, who remained perfectly still, who did what was indicated to her and who sobbed into her pillow when he padded out in his bare feet, not their father, but a grotesque monster.

Veronica told her he had 'done that' to her since she was a child – '*Daardie* terrible things'. She'd learned, as her mother and sister had learned before her, that if she accepted and acquiesced, her father would be satisfied. There would be a semblance of peace in the house.

But there was no real peace. The woman and her daughters were terrified.

Of his fists.

Of his belt.

Of his hard shoes that kicked out at the slightest provocation.

Minnie was born into this. She knew no other way.

When her turn came, she did not understand what her father was doing to her. Or why. But she was used to the silence. The unquestioning acceptance. The shut-down emotions. Because no matter how upset they were, they were not allowed to cry in front of him. Tears brought a violent reaction. A hard slap across the face. An excruciating kick to the shin.

They swallowed their tears. Remained poker-faced.

Sometimes, their father brought them a jug of ginger beer and ice cream from the corner café, and, with jocularity, poured them each a glass of the drink.

They permitted themselves to smile back at him and put their hands together as if in prayer and say, '*Dankie, Pa. Baie danki*e,' and drink without spilling.

He did not like mess. '*Lekker*', he would say, the foam forming a white moustache across his top lip.

'*Ja, Pa. Baie lekker. Dankie.* Yes, Dad. Very nice. Thank you.'

The corner café was the meeting place for the Red Stars Gang. Each called the other 'bro', smoked dagga, drank cheap wine, carried knives or screwdrivers, wore knuckledusters, kicked the dust and watched out for Dago.

Dago was their leader. Tall and lean, with slicked black hair, jutting cheekbones, thickly fringed dark eyes and defined cheekbones. With smooth light skin, with graceful rangy movement, he was, on the surface, beautiful.

But Dago did crazy things. On the spur of the moment, he'd throw petrol over a skulking dog and set it alight. He'd insert a firecracker rocket into the anus of a cat, put a burning match to it and watch the screaming animal being blown to bits, smiling as bits of fur and flesh flew onto his friends. He boasted that could kill sixty penguins in sixty seconds just by twisting their necks.

Dago cared even less about people. People were wary of him. They said he was bad news. He would end up in jail. Or in a back lane with a bullet in his head.

But Dago heeded no one. He swaggered. He swore. He ran the blade of his knife along his finger. He was revered. He was feared. He spoke first. He smiled first. He kept the gang in tense limbo.

Dago could turn like a snake. '*Dago's bad, hy's a bad ou.*'

But it was a good life. Lively. Special wit' Dago.

One of his boasts was virgins. 'I like to break 'em in. Like horses. They can look like a horse as long as they intac'.'

Intact was a word he applied to every girl that passed. 'What you think? Intac'?'

'Only one way to know,' they'd reply, waiting for him to smile.

'That's right,' came the grin. 'Don' mind if I do...'

But Dago did not 'break 'em in' as often as he bragged, because he did not like having sex.

With his pretty face, his father had referred to him as queer, calling him a 'little *moffie*' to whoever would listen, but not for a moment actually believing that he was one. He rough-tumbled with him, taught him how to fight dirty, how to handle a knife. He punched and bruised him into a punched-up bruised teenager, awakening immense hate in the boy. He brought him to a point where Dago felt nothing, and wanted nothing except to hurt others.

But he did harbour a secret. He did hide a deep hurt. What his father did not want to believe was so. He *was* homosexual.

Today, he was bragging about who he 'Took las' night'.

They never questioned him or checked his claims. They would only listen attentively, nod, smirk to match his smirk, admiration for their leader glowing in their eyes.

At dusk on Friday, Minnie walked to the corner shop to buy a bag of rice. Dago was there, leaning against the wall, drawing patterns in the dust with the heel of his shoe. He glanced at her, asked her name, asked where she lived.

She tried to pass by without answering.

'*Hy meisie*, are you deaf?' he demanded. 'I'm speaking to you! What's your name?' He stretched his arm across the shop entrance, leaned towards her, smiled his startling smile, and with his other hand smoothed his hair.

Frightened, she told him.

'What? Speak up. I can' hear what you say.' His tone changed, becoming jocular. Combing his hair with delicate fingers, he leaned in the doorway, his hip jutting. 'Not so fast. I want to speak to you.' He laughed. 'Don' be frighten'. I don' bite. *Ek is nie 'n hond nie.* I'm not a dog.'

He leaned forward until their faces almost touched. 'Do you know who I am?'

She felt his menace.

She looked down.

She saw his tan and white shoes.

'I'm asking you, Dumbo. Do you know my name?'

She knew who he was but her mouth was dry. Her throat choked up and she whispered, '*Nee. Ek weet nie.*'

'Doesn' matter who I is. *Maar jy's pragtig jy weet.* Very pretty. How old are you?'

*Vierteen. Ek is vierteen.* My birthday was las' month.'

'*Vierteen.* Only fourteen.' Dago assessed her. 'So, Minnie. How would you like to come out with me?' He stared into her face.

She lifted her gaze to meet his, saw his burning eyes, his mouth, the copper smoothness of his taut skin. Her gaze fell away and he noted with disdain her dark skin, the *kril* of her hair, her broad nose. But she was 'almos' hunnert percen' a virgin. He could tell his gang about her, how she pursued him, begged him to do it, and he – 'in my most obliging manner' – obliged.

He was surprisingly gentle with her.

In the melancholy dusk of his bedroom, in his empty house on a Saturday afternoon, she watched his closed eyes with their thickly fringed lashes, his delicate eyebrows, the curve of his lips, the fine outline of his jaw, the way his sleek hair fell forward. She felt his tongue in her mouth and the hard driving force of his bony hips against hers.

Passively she waited as he slowly and painfully came inside her.

She was indeed a virgin. With satisfaction, he noted a small spread of blood that had stained his sheet.

He said as he zipped up his jeans, 'I'll have to wash that.'

That was all it was. A brief moment on a lumpy mattress in a gloomy room late on a Saturday afternoon behind torn net curtains.

He never acknowledged her again. Never looked her way. But his friends looked. She felt their smirks as she walked past. Felt the blood rise hotly in her face.

The girl had all the symptoms. Her menstrual periods, that had only started a few months before, stopped. She was nauseous in the mornings. Her breasts were tender and she wanted to cry without knowing why. Her body had changed.

Her mother noticed the slight bulge of her belly. She took her to the bathroom and ordered her to strip. Instinctively, she raised her hand. Minnie's head reeled from a hard slap to her face. Through closed eyes, she saw the horror in her mother's expression, her eyes bulging, bubbles of spit in the corner of her mouth.

'Minnie! *Jy's* pregnant! *My Ghott! My liewe Ghott!*'

The girl hung onto the basin with the backs of her hands, leaned against it to prevent herself from falling. She stared, uncomprehending. The bathroom closed in on her. She felt herself slipping into a grey space.

'*Jy's* pregnant!' Rough hands felt her belly. '*My Here! Wat het jy gedoen?*' The woman's voice rose. 'Minnie! *Se vir my! Met wie het jy gegaan?*'

Minnie swayed in the grey mist of her mind. What did her mother mean? How was she pregnant? Who had she gone with? She'd forced herself to forget the incident with Dago. Now it loomed before her huge and hateful. It filled her with dread.

Another hard slap jerked her into reality. '*Wie was dit!* Tell me! Who did you fuck with! Minnie! Answer me!'

'*Ek weet nie Ma.* I don' know…'

'You don' know! You don' know who made you like this? What are you? Stupid? A piece of rubbish? *My Ghott!* Your father will kill you! You know that! He will kill you! *Hy sal donner jou tot jy dood is*!'

'Ma. *Asseblief se niks vir hom.* Please. Please. Don' tell him.'

'I don' tell him! He will see. He will see with his own eyes. *Dan sal* the shit hit the fan! Oh *my liewe Ghott! Wat sal ons doen?*' Her tone changed from anger to fear.

She sank onto the side of the bath, grasping the girl's arms in her hands. 'What can we do? *Ek moet dink.* I mus' think this through. *My Ghott!* Help me. *Wat kan ons doen…*'

She thought of the hospital. She thought of the doctor. She shook her head in despair. The hospital would chase them away. So would the doctor. They wouldn't help. They can't help. They don't do abortions.

'*My Ghott!* What can we do?'

Then she remembered Sophie, the woman who lived two streets away. She did abortions. A lot of them went to her. She also recalled the two girls who'd died – one who could not stop bleeding, the other who had blood poisoning. But there were others that she'd helped. The ones who were OK. Her mother said to herself, They were mos' OK. They came through…

'*Kom,* Minnie,' she muttered through clenched teeth. '*Kom met my.*'

They walked quickly through the hobbled streets. The sun stung them. There was no movement in the air. Only thick heat.

Minnie had no thoughts. She could not feel her feet on the ground. She moved in the shadow of her mother, following her vague image, her blurred shape.


Sophie, in a faded housecoat and slippers, her hennaed hair pinned untidily on her head, was sweeping her front *stoep.* The moles on her face stood out to greet them.

'Sophie –' the mother tried to say.

The woman glanced up then carried on sweeping. 'I know why you're here. I can see.'


On a grey blanket on a hard bunk in a back room that smelled of stale air, she estimated the pregnancy to be about four months.

'Can you do it?' The mother's hands twisted together. Her shoulders hunched forward. Her face was grey.

'It's a bit far but I can mos' try…'

'*Hoeveel will dit kos?*'

'R120.'

'So *veel…*?'

'*Dis* my price. Take or leave.' Her hands were on her hips. She was in charge. This was her business.

There was a slight hesitation. Then, 'OK. We'll take.'

'Firs' you mus' pay.'

With a sharp intake of breath, the mother drew a tightly rolled bundle of notes from between her breasts, money painstakingly saved to buy a new sofa, and, spitting on her forefinger, counted the notes.

Then Sophie counted it.

'How? How do you do it?' The mother's words were tortured. Her eyes were pinpoints.

'With a knitting needle. To break the waters. To bring on the labours. It won' be easy. She's quite far. But we can *maar* jus' try…' Sophie had pushed up her sleeves and was scrubbing her hands.

Overwhelmed, the mother stared at her terrified daughter and begged of the woman in the overall, '*Sal sy* OK *wees? Na die* abortion *ek bedoel.* Please tell me, will she be OK?'

'*Ek kannie se. Ons sal maar* try…' Not all abortions work, she said. Sometimes there are complications. She was not a miracle worker. But she would do her best. '*Dit sal 'n bietjie seer wees,*' she told Minnie. '*Jy moet net vysbyt…* It will hurt. You must bite hard.'

The girl lay with her face to the wall. A grey watermark in the paint faced her. It was shaped like a spider. She shut her eyes against the ghastly image, clenched her fists, clenched her teeth. Between her legs, she felt the long needle being inserted. She bit her lip until it bled and moved her head from side to side in agony. Moaning softly, she clenched her fists so tight that her nails made deep indents into the palms of her hands.

When she could no longer bear it, when the blood drained from her face and she felt herself losing consciousness, a warm gush of fluids flowed from her vagina and drenched the towel between her legs.

'*Dis goed. Die* waters *het gebreek. Nou moet die* labours begin…'

It took three hours, three agonising hours of increasing waves of pain, becoming one excruciating contraction pushing against the next, becoming one continual wave of red hot pain.

Then, with the help of Sophie pushing hard against her abdomen, a small foetus appeared, fitting into Sophie's broad hand.

'Dis a boy,' she said. '*Wil jy dit sien?*'

The girl nodded. She stared at the perfectly formed baby, at the few strands of black hair. '*Hy's pragtig. So pragtig…*' she whispered. '*Is hy dood?* He's beautiful. So beautiful. Is he dead?'

'*Hy's dood,*' said the woman. '*Nou moet ons die anner uitneem…*'

Minnie lay unmoving, numb and drained as Sophie pushed painfully against her belly until the afterbirth came away. Staunching the flow of blood with *lappies,* she said, '*Dis klaar. Alles is uit. Dis goed. Alles is goed.* It's done. Everything is out. It's all good.'

She glanced at the white face of the girl, at the crumpled face of her mother, and, in an unexpected show of kindness, offered to make them tea with lots of sugar. 'Res' a *bietjie,*' she urged Minnie. 'Lie there a bit. Till you feel better…'

Legally, Minnie is married. Neither she nor her husband ever bothered with divorce.

Jacob was a friend of her father's who came to the house from time to time – who was invited on Christmas Day for a *braai* with his four children. His wife had died giving birth to the youngest.

In his introverted way, Jacob sat in the yard, his back to a wall, watching bubbles rising in his beer glass. He watched the people. Listened to their talk. Heard them laugh. He watched the children tearing wrapping from their gifts, heard their shouts of glee. He watched Minnie.

He wandered into the kitchen, opened another beer, leaned against the wall, saw her chop tomatoes and cucumbers and sprinkle the vinegar. He watched her grate carrots and cabbage and pour the mayonnaise. He saw her prepare the *snoek* for the *braai* and prick the *boerevors* until the juices ran. Saw her thoroughly wipe the surfaces until they were spotlessly clean and wash her hands with vigour and shake them dry. He liked the way her hands worked. Quick. Clean. No fuss.

She gave no indication that she knew he was there, against the wall, watching. She kept her eyes down. Never spoke. But felt the heat rise in her face.

He noticed that it was Minnie who came out to pick up the paper cups and torn wrapping paper, who brought the beers and took away the empties, who served the food and took the dirty plates. He noted the frizz of her hair, her coarse dark skin, her broad nose, her open nostrils. He saw her shy eyes, her hand that quickly came up to hide her smile. Heard her soft voice for the children. Saw them look up at her quizzically, and accept from her sausages and cool drinks, and cake packed with currents.

He noticed the crease between her large breasts, the narrowness of her waist. The lightness with which she walked. Unnoticed. Unobtrusive. A shadow in the crowd.

Only her hands were busy.

She was seventeen, and seventeen years younger than him when he proposed. Her father was pleased to agree. His younger daughter was unattractive. Silent and withdrawn, her only redeeming feature was her ability to clean. That's when she seemed to come alive, when she was scrubbing and wiping, when she was washing or drawing a hot iron across the clothes, when she was scraping the vegetables, or scouring fat from the pans. Marriage to Jacob seemed a good idea. She would be a mother to his children, a scrupulous housekeeper, a quiet and obedient wife. From his daughter's point of view, she would have a man who earned a good living as an upholsterer and lived in a nice house in Wynberg.

There were married at the magistrates court on a Wednesday morning. He wore a suit, she a blue rayon dress with a small corsage pinned to her lapel. They drove back to the plain white house below the railway line with its wire fence and patch of flat green lawn. Jacob immediately changed into overalls and left for work. Minnie folded the marriage certificate and put it in a safe place, changed into a housecoat, hung up the blue rayon dress, put the corsage in a small bowl of water and went to the kitchen.

It was a spacious room. From the window, the sun cast a block of light over a green vinyl table surrounded by wooden chairs and cupboards painted white. A double sink was under the window and next to it a large stove. Green linoleum covered the floor and from a basket in a corner a cat stretched and purred, its tail curled.

She opened the cupboards and found a set of plain white crockery and pots and pans and a stainless steel set of cutlery. There were drinking glasses and white mugs, a big brown teapot and a matching milk jug.

In the fridge were peanut butter and cheese, jams and anchovy paste, milk and yoghurt, an assortment of vegetables and fruit. In the freezer, sealed mincemeat and chicken.

Off the kitchen was a laundry. She found brushes and brooms and floor polish and furniture polish, and window cleaning liquid. She found lots of *lappies*. She found laundry powder and laundry soap and scouring powder for the baths and basins.

She opened the door to the lounge. It was small, more like a parlour, with a green sofa along one wall and two matching armchairs. The curtains, heavy and lined, were drawn, and the windows shut. The smell was stale and slightly mouldy. Minnie wanted to draw back the curtains, to open the windows, let the sun and air in. But then she withdrew. Instinctively. Left it as it was. Closed the door behind her.

She went down the passage to the main bedroom. A double bed was covered with a woven spread in shades of blue. A dressing table matched the bed and built in cupboards lined the wall. Curtains and nets hung at the windows. She saw that the curtains and the bed cover were of the same material. In each of the children's bedrooms were two beds covered in the same blue weave, as were the curtains. It occurred to her that Jacob might have got the roll of woven blue material cheap from a fabric factory. The last remaining yards of a discontinued line.

She went into the bathroom. A shower was installed over the bath, which was surrounded by a striped blue plastic curtain. A toilet in the corner. A row of ornamental wall tiles surrounded the vanity.

She walked through the house again, this time slowly, taking in the shape of it.

In the yard she discovered another toilet, an outside toilet.

Minnie thought, This is a nice house. It's big. It's got big rooms. Nice big windows. It's got light.'

She touched the walls. The walls are nice, she thought. Painted nice. It has a nice wood floor. I like this house, she thought.

A feeling came to her. Stirred inside her. If she was able to recognise it, she would have known that she what she was feeling was a stir of happiness.

She got out the polish and the *lappies*.

The house gleamed. The windows winked. The *imbiua* dining

room table and the sideboard glowed. The silver candlesticks shone brightly. Facets of a cut-glass bowl refracted into rainbows of colour. The linoleum was lighter, brighter – seemed more lively.

Each morning, Minnie polished the three red cement steps to the front door and the red tiles of the little *stoep*.

She polished the brass door knocker.

A sparkling sheen covered every surface.

Sunshine burst from every corner.


She found two char jobs for white women above the railway line in the luxurious suburb of Kenilworth.

Most of what she earned went into a building society account and she hid the savings book in the same place as the marriage certificate. To be fair to him, Jacob never wanted to know what she did with her money. He was a steady earner. Always provided for the needs of the children. Was never unreasonable about what was needed in the house. He noticed that for herself Minnie bought very little. She made do with what she had.

On weekdays, the children walked to the local school. In the afternoons, they were now greeted with the welcoming smells of freshly baked biscuits or, perhaps, fish curry, or a bean and knuckle bone soup bubbling on the stove.

They liked coming home to Minnie. They would sit at the kitchen table doing their homework while she prepared supper or sewed buttons onto their shirts. They liked to watch her darn a sock by pushing a tennis ball into the sock and against the hole. They liked to watch the hole gradually disappear.

Minnie was a quiet and soothing presence. Sometimes she sang softly, sweetly. They listened to her songs and always asked for their favourite – 'Somewhere Over the Rainbow'.

A feeling of serenity flowed through the house. A quiet and gentle peace.

Minnie, for her part, did everything she could for them, except to try to be their mother. She knew that they would not like that. They had photographs of their mother in their bedrooms. They only had one mother, even though she was no longer with them. Even though she was dead. There was no room in their lives for another.

The evenings were even quieter. Jacob was sometimes surly, always taciturn, while she, Minnie, was naturally silent. The radio spoke to them or filtered music through the lounge room. There were cups of tea, a biscuit or two, a cigarette end glowing.

It was in their bedroom that Jacob found his satisfaction with her. She was not unattractive in the dark. He liked the feel of her full breasts and the small of her back. Her body was soft and smooth and she responded to all his demands. At first he used condoms. He did not want another mouth to feed. But after a few months he became careless. He needn't to have been concerned. She did not fall pregnant. The sharp needle that had been inserted into her, that had twisted and probed her, had relentlessly destroyed those parts of her that made babies.

She was forever scarred by the workings of a knitting needle. She would never have a child.

The scene seemed to fit together, the solid breadwinner, the conscientious housewife, four well behaved children.

There was the security of a nice house, a fridge filled with good food, a van to drive to the beach on Sundays, the church on the next corner.

The sun over the Hottentots Holland range was already hot in the early morning. It proceeded to burn away the day.

The air evaporated. There was no movement in the trees, no sign of birds. Waves of heat rose from the roads, releasing the acrid smell of melting tar.

From the kitchen window, Minnie saw the neighbour's chrysanthemums bend their heavy blue heads against the merciless shafts of sun, their blossoms crisping, their leaves curled down.

The children were listless.

I will take them to the beach, she thought.

She packed sandwiches, biscuits and a bag of yellow cling peaches.

They caught the train to Muizenberg. Excited and exuberant, they fought to sit next to the windows.

'*Biy stil*,' she had to say. '*Haai* man! Don' kick your feet…'

It was a long way from the station to the Coloured beach. They walked past the Snake Park.

'That's where the Jew people go,' she told them.

Past the Christian beach.

'That's for the other whites, the Christians,' and she pointed to the signs 'Whites Only'.

Jacob's son spat at the sign.

'*Haai!*' exclaimed Minnie.

'*My Pa* say I mus' spit at these signs,' he answered sullenly.

Further along the road was their designated stretch of sand and sea.

'*Luister mooi nou* – mus' swim on'y by the flags,' she instructed as they ran to the water.

Tired from the heat and the long walk, Minnie sank down onto the sand. It was warm and fine and white. She stretched her legs, rubbed her calves, flexed her feet.

She watched the children jump in the waves, heard their yells, their laughter.

She looked beyond them and saw the sea meeting the horizon. In the far distance was Gordon's Bay, a hazy outline of seaside cottages against the unblemished sky.

*Dis a blou dag*, she thought. A blue day. *Blou is ook a mooi kleur*, she said to herself. Blue is also a pretty colour…

There was no movement in the air. There was no shade. The sun beat on her shoulders. Her forehead was beaded with sweat. She pushed herself up and walked to the water. The children were like little seals, their brown bodies glistening as they dived under the waves.

'Aunty,' they grinned, '*Dis so lekker. Die* water's so warm.'

Her feet squelched in the soft wet sand and forced itself between her toes. Ripples of water moved coolly around her ankles. She'd not been in the sea since she was a child. It felt alive, the shifting sand, the moving surf. She lifted her skirt, tucked it into the elastic of her panties and walked further into the water.

'*Kom binne*, Aunty. *Dis so mooi,*' sang the children.

The waves broke against her legs, against her dress. She splashed her arms, her face, the back of her neck.

A big wave took her by surprise, wetting her to her waist.

'*Ag wat!*' she gasped and then she laughed and threw herself into the foamy white surf. She waded in until she felt the crash of the swells. She jumped each high wave and swam towards the next one.

In the rhythm of the waves and the cold wet of the water, she felt free and filled with joy. Against the crashing sound of the sea, she was uninhibited. Unafraid.

She threw her head back, threw her arms in the air and laughed aloud.

The sweet tones of her voice filtered through the blue air as she sang, 'You are my sunshine, my only sunshine, You make me happy when skies are blue.'

She'd planted a bed of bulbs given to her by the neighbour.

He told her how to plant them, what roots faced downwards in the ground, what needed to face upwards, towards the surface.

He gave her food for the young plants.

From this bed came a riotous mass of colours from anemones, ranuncula and freesia, and such wonderful perfumes that hosts of bees visited the blooms each day, unable to stay away .

Time passed. Months became years.

Minnie was getting on Jacob's nerves. Her long silences, her acquiescence, her unquestioning acceptance of all things began to irritate him and he deliberately found fault in order to illicit some reaction. There was none.

She even apologised for things she was accused of that she did not do.

It was insidious. At first a push, a shove, a rough brushing by. A hard slap on her hand, a slap across her back.

'*Haai* man! *Moenie!*' she protested but he glared at her until she had to drop her eyes and turn away.

She became silent.

No longer sang.

No longer watered the flowers.

He punched her hard in the chest. She ran from him into the bedroom and locked the door. He banged and kicked and swore and cursed until she, terrified, opened it. He came at her with all his height and weight. She was almost unconscious by the time he pulled himself off her, leaving her with a bleeding and broken nose, blackened eyes, a cracked cheekbone, a bruised and battered body. She crawled into a ball and remained in a corner of the room throughout the night.

The children had huddled in the passage, their fists stuffed into their mouths, their eyes round with fear.

The next morning, the madness that had overcome him subsided. He helped her to her feet, assisted her to the bathroom and washed the dried blood from her face. He said he was sorry. Mumbled that it would never happen again.

He made her and the children swear they would not talk about it, not to anyone.

She promised.

The children promised.

Her body mended, her bones knitted, and the bruises faded, but she could not come to terms with what had happened.

She'd taken punishment as a child blamed for things she did not do. Had never been able to ask why.

But now she could question. Why? For what? What had she done?

She'd tried so hard. Worked so hard to make it nice. The house. The children. Make their food. Wash their clothes. Look after them when they feel sick. Look at their homework. Listen to their stories.

Something shattered within her. Something intractable. Irreparable.

She was filled with cold. With hard.

She pushed through the days, cleaned, polished, washed, ironed. Drove herself until she became exhausted.

She made herself a promise. She told herself that she'd taken a lot of punishment in her life. And what for? She promised herself that she would no longer take punishment.

She's *mos* a person also!

She's *mos* a human being!

She's not a dog!

Not a *fokken* bladdy dog.

She promised herself, '*Nee man*. No more.'


He broke his word. A drink too many did it. This time she yelled back at him, boldly took the blows, until one punch to the head sent her reeling blackly into a wall.

On a silent sunny morning, she packed a suitcase and left, taking her savings book.

She went up the street with measured steps.

Away from that family.

From that house.

Away from the years she'd spent there.

In the kitchen on the green vinyl table in the centre of a white saucer lay her thin gold wedding band. The marriage certificate remained in its hidden place, where it would never be found.

Dana sipped her tea in the filtered light of early morning. In the tumble of bed linen, her hair spread dark on a silken pillow, she stretched herself like a cat, relishing the smoothness of her skin against the silkiness of fine sheets.

It was the time of day that was best for her. Mark and the children gone from the house. Minnie downstairs. The dog quiet. Only the movement of voile curtains in a gentle breeze and the perfume of yesterday's roses.

Dana was not a peaceful person. She surprised herself that she was able to relax in this way. Sometimes she thought that she was not relaxing. She was hiding. From Mark. From the children. From her life. But, she chided herself, she had always been this way. When she was a child. When she was growing up. Hiding. Shrinking. They used to call her shy. Smile at her with fondness, ruffle her hair and say that she was shy. But clever.

This was how her world knew her. Clever but shy.

Dana was not shy. She was withdrawn.

Lettie had been her nanny from the time she was born. A large woman with ample breasts and a huge backside enough to seat a child. A woman with a dark round face, black round eyes, a white smile and a laugh that came from her belly.

There's a photograph of Dana sitting in a pram, dressed in white with a white beret on her dark curls. Holding the handle of the pram is Lettie, glowing in a white overall, starched and pleated apron and starched cap hiding her woolly head. She is smiling her bright white smile. Dana doesn't smile.

The large native woman. The small white child.

Lettie could be jolly. She would jiggle her huge behind to the beat of native music, moving lightly on her feet with the natural rhythm of her people. She could laugh and show love to baby Dana to the delight of her mother and father.

She was able to charm the uncles and the aunts. They loved to make Lettie laugh. She loved to make them laugh.

That was Lettie. The one they thought they knew.

But Lettie had a dark side. Darker than the colour of her skin. Brought on by the darkness of her own life.

Her hard dark life – a child of the location.

Hard earth.

Harsh voices.

Sharp smacks.

Poverty.

Hunger.

Deprivation.

Then finally salvation. A job for 'poor whites' as a domestic in a small country *dorp*.

Age? Eleven.

Hard. Very hard.

But at least there was a mattress to sleep on, and bread and jam and mealie meal. However badly her impoverished employers treated her – her paltry salary, the long hours of physical work, the lack of regard or respect for her – all of this was better than her life in the location.

But the job had further consequence on her psyche.

She was now in touch with whites. In their home. Suffering their ill-treatment of her.

In this place she learned another lesson. How to hate whites.


Lettie moved from job to job, up the line, so to speak, getting fat and jolly on mounds of bread and jam, porridge and mealie meal. She ate copiously, trying to fill the big black hole that was always inside her.

She learned to laugh.

She jiggled to her music.

She had sex.

She hoped for love.

Was abused by the men in her life.

Pushed.

Punched.

They stole her heart.

They stole her money.

She had one child. A daughter. Brought up by an old woman in the location whom she paid. Sometimes she saw the child. Sometimes she didn't.

She frightened Dana on nights when the parents went out. She'd make noises in the dark. Go outside and knock on the window. Said that there was a *tokeloshe* – frightening superstitious talisman – under the bed. Told her that the boogie man was coming to get her.

The small girl would bury her head under her blanket, cover her ears with her little hands and scream silently into her pillow.

Lettie would pull the blanket off her, hit the soles of her little feet with a ruler and hiss, 'If you tell your mommy that the boogie man comes, tomorrow I will be very bad to you.'

In the bright light of day, the nanny smiled her white smile and called the child Danie. She gave her fudge from her apron pocket. Her mother would laugh and say that Lettie spoilt her. Gave her too many sweets. But she was pleased to have such a kind and jolly nanny for their cherished child.

Dana's parents wished that she would talk more. 'She's so shy,' they would say softly and with affection. 'She really needs to come out of her shell.'

She was a clever child with an excellent memory. When her father read her stories, she remembered when to turn the pages although she was herself was not yet reading. She would whisper reams of nursery rhymes off by heart. She would count and add and subtract her uncle's fingers.

'How many?' He would ask with a blustering laugh, holding up his big hairy fingers.

She knew the answers. Free. Or six. Or nine.

'So clever,' they would say and applaud, and brush up her dark curls and kiss her on her round pink cheeks.

'So shy,' they would say…

Lettie was a constant threat in Dana's life. A dark and lurking shadow that the child had shrunk from and, in so doing, shrunk from everyone else.

But now she was seven. She was beginning to grow away from the nanny's moods, her smile, her jolly laugh, and the dark and ugly side of her. She was able to look at the nanny's gleaming bovine face, at her round dark eyes, at her punishing hands, and not look down.

The nanny sensed this. She realised it was time to go.

But all that was a long time ago.

Lettie was dead.

Only her legacy remained.


Dana ran her fingers through her hair. She'd have to speak to Jono. The whole of last week her hair looked lousy. Just hung. The sides are too long. And maybe a bit of a colour. He needs to fix it. Thinking about her hair, about the hairdresser, gave her impetus to throw the coverings from her, to pull off her pyjamas and, naked and on the balls of her feet, go to the bathroom.

Her reflection watched her in the full-length mirror. Her long legs, still shapely despite their thinness, her skinny arms, her bony shoulders. She stood sideways and sucked in her breath to find her ribcage. Her stomach, she was pleased to see, concaved. And there were her hip bones. The scale said just under fifty kilos. They all thought she was too thin, but, she thought, pinching her skin, she could lose another kilo or two.

Mark asked her what the hell she thought she was doing, that she'd had a much better figure when they married. At least she'd had some flesh on her. She took no notice of him. She told them all she felt fine, that she was eating well, that this was a natural weight for her. But truth be told, these days she never felt hungry. She had to remind herself to eat.

She dressed, leaving discarded clothes on the bed and her bottles of face creams and make-up scattered on the dressing table. Casting one last flash of her face in the mirror, she pinched her cheeks, threw her bag across her shoulder and ran lightly down the stairs, her pink silk scarf flowing and a trail of Shalimar following her.

'Minnie,' she spoke to the broad back of the maid, 'I'm off. I'll bring the *kitkes* and the other stuff for the salads. Is there anything else we need?'

'No *Merrem*. We got everything.'

'OK then. So you'll do the chopped herring and the *perogen*. You might as well stew the apples this morning and put them in the fridge. Put a bit of lemon in. Oh yes. And lay the table. Nine places. Zaidah isn't coming.'

She waited for Minnie to turn round. 'What else? Leave the flowers. I'll do them when I get back.'

Thinking aloud, she said, 'The chicken's ready. The couscous you'll do just before they come. Minnie, don't forget the mushrooms. For the couscous.'

'Yes *Merrem*.'

'And please see that the silver is cleaned. Properly. I can't stand those little black marks on the forks.' She studied the maid's face. She could not read it. Something's going on with her, Dana thought. She paused. She wondered.

'And set the table.'

'You tol' me already,' the maid grumbled silently.

Dana lifted her bag onto her shoulder. Then, without turning back, she called, 'And do the serviettes in those nice standing-up shapes. Like you did last time.'

Minnie saw the pink scarf flounce out of the kitchen. She took a deep breath, leaned against the sink. Waited.

The house needed to settle.

In the kitchen, the comforting smell of cooking. Garden perfumes through the windows. Outside, the insistent call of a bird. The leaves of the plane trees brushed together. Somewhere a tap dripped.

Then, overwhelmed with panic, Minnie rushed to unlock the door of her room. The air was thick and stale, the bed untidy, a half-filled cup of cold tea on the table.

She felt for the package, took it out, unwrapped it, flicked through the notes, wrapped it and put it back.

Relieved and afraid, she wondered whether she should go down to the bus shelter again. To see if anyone was there. If anyone was searching.

'*Haai* man!' she admonished herself.

Thoughtlessly she moved through the house dusting, sweeping, polishing and wiping. Chopped and sliced and stirred and tasted without tasting.

She cleaned the cutlery and set the pieces on the table as she had been trained, left to right, right to left. Rainbows broke on chiselled crystal, knife handles glowed and the starched linen serviettes stood up in points. *Merrem* will examine it. She will make straight a fork and move a glass and put the flowers and the candles and say it looks beautiful.

But Minnie had no appreciation of fine linen or solid silver or cut glass. She unpacked the things, laid them out.

Later. Much later.

Wash them.

Dry them.

Sort the cutlery.

Stack the dishes.

Rub the crystal glasses.

Pack it all away.

The house glowed with Shabbat. A mantle of love and warmth accompanied a mellow mood of soft smiles and gentle eyes.

The children came with special decorum, their faces polished, the boys in crisp shirts with hair slicked, the girls in pretty dresses with hairstyles held with fancy pins, in deference to Shabbat.

The word was deference. In the muted light of chandeliers, in the flicker of Shabbat candles, an unknown presence held everyone to account. There was something bigger than them on Shabbat. They felt it and were happy to submit to it.

Not experiencing the reverence was Minnie waiting in the kitchen ready to serve. She heard the voices, the greetings and the laughter. Thinking of the long evening ahead, she wished herself far away from this *fokken* night where they ate so late with all the different courses from the chopped herring to the soup to the meat to the pudding. And carrying the heavy tray to the table. Up an' down. Up an' down. And all the dirty plates and all the dirty knives and forks and glasses, to wash, to dry, to pack away, before she finally saw the backs of all of them, with their ten-rand notes folded into her pocket. 'Don't forget to tip the shiksa,' someone would inevitably say. Inevitably she would hear them saying it.

Carmel touched her pearls with lacquered nails and whispered to Sam, 'I think they've painted the walls. It's different. Darker. I'm sure they've redone it…'

'Shut up for Christ's sake!' he muttered, his mind again registering her foolishness. She was going to end up in trouble, the way she watched Dana and what she spent. If Dana got to hear how often Carmel told her sisters that Mark's wife sure knew how to spend his money, Dana would be as mad as all hell. She'd cut them out. They wouldn't be able to come to the house. Did Carmel want that, he'd demanded. Would she be happy if Dana had nothing to do with them? 'And Dana would do it! She'd cut us dead. You know what she's like. No easy baby, that one!'

He left his wife's side to greet Dana's mother and ask after Jack.

'He's still not right,' Granny smiled, her face breaking into lines. 'It's taking a long time. His back's still giving him trouble. That's why he's not here. I told him. Jack, I said, you'd be meshuggah to go out tonight. In and out of the car. Up and down the stairs. He needs to give it another couple of weeks.'

Maralyn and Dave were the last to arrive. They were sorry. Their daughter'd had a nose bleed. No, she was fine, thanks, they said. It's stopped. She gets it from time to time.

'*Kippot?* Have you all got?' Mark straightened Jeremy's kippa that was sitting crookedly over one ear and kept his hands on the boy's shoulders.

Dana covered her eyes and said softly in Hebrew the ancient blessing, 'Blessed are you, God, who has sanctified us with his commandments and commanded us to light the lights of Shabbat.'

It was Mark's turn. 'On the seventh day, God had finished his work which he had made; and he rested on the seventh day from all his work that he had made. And God blessed the seventh day, and he hallowed it, because he rested thereon from all his work which God had created and made. Blessed are you, God, King of the Universe, who made us holy with his commandments and favoured us, and gave us his holy Shabbat, in love and favour, to be our heritage, as a reminder of the Creation. You chose us and made us holy, and you gave us your holy Shabbat, in love and favour, as our heritage. Blessed are you, God, who sanctified Shabbat. Amen.'

The fourth commandment. Every Friday night.

The ten commandments. Thou shalt not...

The wine was passed around in tiny silver goblets and the children blessed the covered plaited bread.

Maralyn leant over the table, her blonde hair catching the light, to smell the roses, to touch one with a small creamy hand, her nails like pink rosebuds. Was it her perfume or the roses, Mark wondered.

'What a beautiful scent they have,' she breathed. 'The roses we buy have no scent at all.'

'My mom…' Dana nodded at her mother. 'She looks after them. Prunes them and feeds them.'

'I love gardening.' Granny's face crinkled. 'Specially roses. I love roses. You have to feed them but you also have to let them rest. Then they give wonderful flowers with beautiful scents.' Her blunt hands held together. They were working hands. Kneading and rolling. Stirring and slicing. Sewing or knitting. Soothing hands. Gentle and helpful. Now resting in the warmth of her lap.

But Carmel thought little of Granny with her industrious ways. She found nothing in common with the plain grey-haired woman in her home-made cardigans who, she claimed, spent her life in her kitchen making cinnamon buns.

'Who eats *bulkes* these days?' she'd demand of Sam, her lips pursed, her eyes pinpointed.

She wondered how Granny had produced a daughter like Dana, so clever and smart, so fashionable, and with such impeccable taste. Where did the girl learn all this, she wondered. Certainly not in her own home. And, bitterly she asked herself, where on earth did she learn to spend money like she did? They never had much money…

'I hear the Segals are leaving.'

'I also heard that. Carly Hassen was talking about it in Shul.'

'Funny. I saw Eric last week and he never said a word about it.'

'Well, what's new? When does anyone tell you if they're leaving? They talk about everyone else but when it comes to themselves they're shtum.'

'You're right,' Mark's father chuckled. 'Shtum as Yourke's *hund*.'

'Where does that saying come from?' Maralyn's thickly fringed turquoise eyes turned him.

'Shtum as Yourke's *hund*?' his grey teeth grinned. 'I'll tell you where it comes from. It comes from *der heim*. It's an old *shtetl* story. From Lithuania. Old Yourke had a dog that used to bark at anything that moved, and also anything that didn't move. It barked all day and all night. Got on the whole village's nerves. But one night when the place was dead asleep a thief managed to get into his yard and steal his cow and his goat and all the chickens. And do you know…' he paused.

'The dog lay there watching the thief and not a sound came out of him, not even the whisper of a bark. The thief got away with the whole caboodle and the dog lay quiet as a lamb, just watching. Boy, oh boy, was Yourke mad the next morning when he saw that all his chickens and his goat and his cow were gone! He said to the dog, "You great big stupid dog. Why didn't you warn me?" The dog just wagged its tail and barked at a fly that had come through the window. That's how stupid it was. Barked at a fly but let the thief get away with all the livestock! That's where the saying comes from – Shtum as Yourke's *hund*. Never barked when it should've.' He grinned and wagged his finger at the children.

Mark, irritated, turned the conversation away from his father. 'Where're they going?'

'Carly said to Australia. They've got family there. Her brother and his wife and kids are in Sydney. They left a couple of years ago.'

'Australia. Everybody's going to Australia…'

'No they're not!' piped young Jeremy. 'Brad Stein's going to the USA!'

'The USA?' Mark's father grinned. 'The USA? Tell me, Jeremy. Where's the USA?'

'I know where it is. Brad told me.' The child's words rushed across the table. 'You have to go across the Atlantic Ocean in a plane and then you come to the USA. But your things go in a boat. All their things will be packed in boxes and go in a big, like, something big, and this thing goes onto a boat – I mean a ship – and it goes across to the USA. Then they get their stuff. When the ship comes.'

'So they're going to the States. God knows what his father will do when they get there. He's only ever worked in a job…'

'He's got a brother-in-law there who runs quite a big estate agency business. Maybe he'll work for him.'

'Estate agency? He's never sold anything in his whole life. He's not a salesman's backside.'

'But they've got money.'

'Who knows how much? You've gotta have a lotta boodle in the States. There's no public medical cover. I know a guy who went across with his family. He supposedly had *geld*, bought a house and so on. But when he needed a big op last year, the friends had to have a collection to help him pay for it. No joke. I'm telling you, no joke.'

'Australia has medical cover. The minute you arrive you're covered.'

'Well, that's a big win. But look at the exchange rate. It's a disaster.'

'And try and sell your house here. The Bernsteins got *kadochis* for theirs.'

'Gave it away.'

'And one day we'll have to give South Africa away… The *schwarzes* will take over.'

'That's when the shit'll hit the fan.'

'It could happen.'

'Then watch this place… It'll go only one way and that's down. With the *schwarzes* in charge, can anybody tell me, please, in plain English, what chance has this place got? Zilch!'

'That won't happen. South Africa's too strong for that to happen.'

'Famous last words… I'm telling you, it'll be the end of this place and the end of us. They hate us like poison, those *schwartzes*… They'll do us all in.'

They shifted uncomfortably in their seats. The children were quiet, too quiet and Dana asked quickly who would like more soup. Another *perog*? And called for Minnie to take the soup plates.

The maid caught bits and pieces of the conversation, none of which mattered to her. She'd heard that the Segals were leaving and that they'd fixed their maid up to work for a relative. The maid was satisfied with it because it was a flat. Better *mos* than the big house with the upstairs and the downstairs, and git the same money.

Minnie'd also heard *Merrem* an' *Mastah* talk about this leaving business and *Mastah* git cross 'n' shout, 'Leave me alone! I'm going nowhere! I've got a business to run! That's all I'm thinking about. I'm not going anywhere!'

'So,' drawled Mark, his knife clutched in his fist, the blade facing the ceiling, 'you guys looking forward to Plett this year?'

Maralyn said yes, they were. Taking the same house as last year.

'So are we…'

'You know what we're doing, Mark,' Dana fixed her gaze on him. Her voice was flat. 'We do the same every year…'

'Cool it, Dana,' Mark drawled, his dark eyes flickering over Maralyn's face. 'I'm just making conversation. That's all. Making conversation…'

Minnie cleared the table and salted and soaked the wine stains on the cloth. She counted the cutlery and thought that it was right but Madam found a fish fork to be missing.

'Nobody goes to bed until we find it,' said Madam aloud to herself and for Minnie to hear.

The maid looked under the table and in the bin that stood in the kitchen. She went down the dark path to the big bins and scrabbled through the plastic bags. She felt through bits of food and vegetable peelings and crunched the soiled paper towels, watched in the shadows by a wild cat carved into a statue holding Minnie's hunched form in its hypnotic jade gaze. She found the fork.

Sighing deeply, she walked slowly back to the kitchen, took her plate from the warmer and, back in her room, kicked off her shoes and took a few mouthfuls of food.

Exhausted, she felt for the roll of money, pulled on her nightie, stretched out on the bed and instantly fell into a deep sleep.

Christmas strung across the shops in tinsel and reindeer, and in their windows were grouped Christ-in-the-manger figurines. Branches smelling of pine were piled on pavement corners to be bought and dressed and placed in tangles of lights in front windows, to know that it was Christmas.

Minnie walked past the Stuttafords windows, not seeing them. The store was out of her realm, another world. She was on her way to the OK Bazaars to buy Christmas presents.

But when she got to the corner to cross the main road to the OK Bazaars, she paused. A thought came to her. The money…

She thought about Stuttafords.

Thought about the money.

All that money…

*Her* money…

She stood still, stared ahead, and thought that she could go to Stuttafords. *Sommer* to jus' go there and look. Jus' to look. Jus' to see what there is. How much it cost…

She could go to Stuttafords. Like *Merrem*.

She had the money.

Akshully, she could buy in that shop…

She walked back and stood hesitating in the entrance in her closed shoes and her comfortable green shopping dress, dazzled by the winter wonderland that faced her. White upon crystal white. Pixellated squares of glass prisms on huge revolving spheres casting snowflakes of light over shop counters. A white reindeer commandeering the floor, its horns glistening with gold dust, its hooves gold.

She surreptitiously noticed tiny silver Christmas trees at each end of each counter and that the shop attendants wore white trimmed with silver. There were fragrances from sample perfume bottles and a woman was gently rubbing cream into the hands of a customer.

'Never use anything else,' Minnie heard her say. 'Sure it costs, but what the hell! There's nothing like it, I swear! I'd never use anything else!'

Overwhelmed, blinded by the store's pristine perfection, she was unsure of what to do next. She moved forward awkwardly, thinking, *Ghott!* What am I doing in this place? Conspicuous, embarrassed, she was sure the assistants were focused on her, that they were thinking, Who is she? Why is she here?

Hesitating, trying to find direction, she thought desperately of maybe a shirt for Devin. She could go to the men's shirts. Jus' *sommer* to look…and managed to get the words out. '*Kan die* missus please tell me where I can find the men's shirts…' Her nails were digging half moons into her palms.

The section for men's clothing was muted, softly brown, and she saw a rack with shirts which said 'Half-price – fifty per cent off! Special pre-Christmas offer!' She stood staring, suddenly not knowing his size. Putting her hand out towards the rack, she pulled back, afraid to touch.

A man in black came and asked did she need any help, madam? Did she have anything in mind? Any particular colour? Size?

All she could do was shake her head. 'Sorry, *meneer*. Sorry. *Ek is nie seker nie. Ek weet nie…*'

Shaken, in a panic, she walked back quickly through the white perfumed light and out to the sunshine, the pavement, the reassuring sound of traffic.

With a profound feeling of intense relief, she crossed to the OK Bazaars, to the crammed rails of cheap clothes, the noisy customers brushing past each other, the loud talk, the sound of a large laugh, of a mother shouting at her child.

Immediately she found the men's shirts. Instantly she knew Devin's shirt size.


Minnie thought that it would be better to do the usual thing with the presents. If she got them better things, more expensive things, the family would want to know how she could pay for them. They would ask where she got the money from.

Maybe they think she pinched it from the old granny's purse.

Maybe she pinch from the *Merrem*.

They would have lots to say.

For sure.

She decided that she would not use any of her treasure on them. She would use the Christmas money she'd saved each month for presents, as she had always done.

Later that evening, with Blackie at her feet, she sat with her knees spread and her face in her hands.

Her thoughts wandered over the day, and an uncomfortableness came from within her. In her mind's eye, she saw the deprecating looks and raised eyebrows of those polished assistants in Perfumery. She visualised the sardonic curl of the lip of the man in the black suit in Men's Shirts, his longness, his leanness, his hair that seemed crafted from plaster and tarred with black.

A dull anger welled in her, making her cheeks dark and warm. The closed space, the dog's breath, both were warm with her.

Angrily she muttered, '*Haai! Fok* them!'

She took a deep breath and leaned back in the chair. Feeling for her money, she again counted the notes.

Akshully, she said to herself, I can go back to that store, to that *fokken* Stuttafords any time. I'm entitle! I got the money, same as anybody else.

I can buy things in that shop same as anyone.

Same as *Merrem*.

Slowly she pushed herself up with legs firmly planted, leaned heavily on the table and stared at the bundle of notes, then said aloud and with measured deliberation, 'Yes. For sure. I can go back there. I got the money.'

She opened the window and pulled back the curtain.

For a few moments, a lick of late sunset painted the room rosy pink.

Christmas at Devin's each year meant a Christmas pudding, made by Minnie, packed with sultanas and spices, *tiekies* and sixpences. It became sticky in the heat on the bus to Bonteheuvel, sugar crystallising on its brown bubbled surface.

Christmas was a *braai* in Devin's yard with the spice of *boerevors*, its fat dripping, and smoking *snoek* and marinaded chicken, pungent smells that made the dogs bark and beg, their tongues dripping in anticipation.

Christmas stretched from the kitchen table to a trestle table in the yard to scattered chairs and cushions, to the children sitting on the kitchen steps hugging their presents. To the beer and the wine, the family, the friends. The laughter. The chatter. The good cheer.

It was a warm day with clear skies. Devin was happy. He kissed his wife on the mouth and smacked her bottom. He winked at his friends.

Sue-Ellen wound silver tinsel around her throat and bracelets of tinsel on her wrists. She was barefoot and drank wine from a bottle and gave out Christmas hats of coloured paper and glowing cone-shaped red and green hats. A Christmas carol crackled from someone's radio, 'Oh come let us adore Him, Oh come let us adore Him, Oh come let us adore Him, Christ the Lord.'

Over the day, the house and yard filled with neighbours and more friends. As the pile of empties grew, the crowd grew louder, the laughter more raucous. A drunk woman danced and sang. In the afternoon, she fell asleep against a wall, dried tears staining her cheeks.

The day became hot. Minnie moved to the shade at the side of the house and found Clementine under her sun hat, her face beaded in sweat, a *boerevors* roll being torn off in big bites by her remaining teeth. Her dress was spattered with crumbs and a smear of mustard had settled on her chin. She clutched a bottle of warm beer.

The two women exchanged kisses and a few words. They were content to sit quietly side by side.

Minnie thought of her sister with her smooth skin and straight hair highlighted with blonde streaks. She was now a Whitey. She would not want to be here, thought Minnie. Not in this place with these Coloured people who were rooted in their ways, in their words. Who understood their own jokes, and also understood when they were not joking. Who drank their wine from bottles and tore pieces of *snoek* with their fingers.

The day trickled away. The sun was in the west and a sea breeze tugged at paper cups and plates scattered on the lawn. An outline of the moon, thin as tissue paper, appeared.

A contented drunken tiredness had descended on the yard as the people gradually drifted away.

Minnie and Devin's boys picked up the mess in the garden and packed away the chairs. She rinsed the dishes and stacked them, did a quick sweep of the floor, kissed the boys, then went down the cracked pavements and caught the last bus to Claremont.

Devin snored on his bed. Sue-Ellen stretched out with glazed eyes on a kitchen chair. The last moments of day blushed in the flare of sunset.

Then dusk came and took the sparkle from the tinsel that fell in long dragging strands from the tree slumped in the window. From its branches, angels and Father Christmases hung disconsolately, waiting to be packed away for another year.

She rose heavily with the sun the day after Christmas.

Stony-faced, she came into the kitchen and switched on the kettle. She had a lot to do. The family were going on holiday.

She moved swiftly through the house, stripping the beds, shutting the windows, drawing the curtains.

She emptied the fridge, taking what she could use – vegetables, bread, the remainder of the chicken casserole. She took the dog's food and washing powder and instant coffee and a handful of teabags. Before they locked the back door, she remembered the sugar.

They took their noise and their luggage and they left. They would be gone for three weeks.

*Merrem*'d had a cut 'n' colour, she noticed. Her hair was blue and her skin was brown. From the fake tan. Funny, thought Minnie darkly. My people want light skin. *They* want brown.

Minnie would have her rest, but she would also look after Blackie, and keep the garden watered.

'I don't want to come home to a dead rose garden!' was *Merrem*'s way of saying goodbye.

The house, now locked and shut off, was silent and lifeless. Blackie, sensing change, ran around the yard like a dog possessed and scratched frantically on the kitchen door. Seeking comfort, he pushed against Minnie's legs. She threatened him with a broom she was using to sweep away fallen fruit.

Then she stood motionless on the path of cracked cement slabs, enveloped by silence. She felt the ominous quiet seeping into her. She stared vacantly at the nothingness of the day.

Disconcerted, she resolved to make a cup of tea. She sat in the shade of the plum trees, slowly sipping the sweet strong beverage, Then she leaned forward with her elbows on her knees. Her face fell. Her cheeks sagged.

She was restless. Ill at ease. Had a need for something to do. Something to wipe down. Something to pick up.

But there was nothing to do.

She faced the emptiness.

The oppressive stillness.

The sullen quiet.

Stretching her legs, she saw that her feet had become fat in the heat.

She rubbed her big fingers. Put her chin in her hands. Sighed.

'*Haai* Blackie,' she said, not to the dog but to herself. '*Hierdie lewe. Dis vragtig nie goed nie…*' It was not a good life.

The dog, looked up, scratched an ear, licked her ankle. Sadly it put its head back between its paws.

But then she remembered. Tomorrow was *Tweede Nuwe Dag*. The second day of the new year. The day of the Coon Carnival.

*Daar kom die Alibama*
*Die Alibama Die Alibama Die Alibama*
*Dar kom die Alibama*
*Die Alibama kom oor die see…*

They were pressed into a crowd in Adderley Street. A woman tried to elbow past them. Minnie stuck out her own elbow and stubbornly stood her ground. No one was going to block her view. She'd pushed the boys to the front. Sue-Ellen was pushed up against her.

They heard the music. The carnival could not be far behind. Here they come!

The minstrels of the Coon Carnival on *Tweede Nuwe Dag* exploded onto the street with the beat of their trombones, their tambourines, their penny whistles and drums. They painted the day in violent purple and brilliant orange and sparkling white, navy and yellow, shocking pinks and reds, sea green and sky blue satin jackets and pants, and matching panama hats, with painted faces, with twirling sparkling batons and with marching dancing feet.

There was Devin in royal blue and white with his Crazy Boys Troupe, his face painted white, one eye ringed in black, with a stripe of red lipstick down each cheek. The boys struggled to recognise him, but they remembered the suit that Sue-Ellen had pinned on him and sewed, and the hat they'd been allowed to try on, cavorting around the house until he took it away.

'There's Daddy!' they screamed.

Devin grinned and waved ecstatically in their direction. Intoxicated by the excitement of the crowd, he played to them as he'd done when he was a child. When he was a small mascot dressed in a miniature satin suit twirling a sparkling baton and leading his father's troupe.

The music beats in his feet, in his hips, in his mouth and into his head. Today he is once again the child. Uninhibited, exuberant, rhythmic, Devin gyrates. Devin sings. He dances and marches. He strums on his banjo. He throws his face upwards to the sky. Today Devin is removed from every other day. Today Devin is crazy with uncontainable joy.

They danced past, the troupes in their colours, on their way to the stadium, cheered by people of all colour. Standing together. Side by side.

*Yirrah! Tweede Nuwe Dag!*

As the last troupe entered the stadium, Minnie heard behind her, 'Yes. Every second day of January. Something to do with they were slaves. I think… They were made to work on New Year and were then given the second of January as their holiday. Do you want to go into the stadium and see who wins? I think there are about forty entrants this year… Coloureds and Malays… They get prizes…'

People crowded onto seats as the troupes danced and marched around the stadium past the table where the judges sat.

It went on into the hot afternoon. The crowd mopped their faces. Their feet were swollen. Their backs ached. The children became irritable.

But they stayed. This day of magic, this musical dancing cavorting day… No one wanted it to end. The sun began to dip into the sea from a red and pink sky.

A transparent moon hung delicately in the distant horizon.

A wind came along, brushing against the waves.

A man sitting on a pavement solemnly played the Last Post.

Paper serviettes and paper cups swirled in the wind and a trampled straw panama hat in red and gold bowled along like a soccer ball.


Minnie got off at Claremont Station, waved at the faces of her family pressed against the window and waited until the train had gone.

She sat down heavily on a bench and took off Granny's sandals. There were blisters on her heels.

With bare feet, she started the walk up the long hill, along the smooth pavements and past the white walls, in the welcome cool of early evening.

Dusk was settling serenely, holding the scent of honeysuckle.

Outside the house, stretched on the pavement, with open eyes and open mouth, was the neighbour's gardener, Jake Mlhanga. An empty bottle lay beside him.

'*Haai* Jake. *Wat doen jy?*'

'Minnie? I'm drunk. New Year…it's a time for drink.' He rolled over and sat, his head in his hands. 'New Year. A time to be happy. To take a drink. To be happy…'

'*Heppy Nuwe Jaar* Jake…'

'Happy. Happy. Happy.' He lifted the bottle to his lips, sucked out the few remaining drops and threw it into the gutter. It broke and shattered into sharp shards of green glass.

'*Haai* Jake. *Jy'd dit gebreek…*'

'Broken bottle. Also broken country.' He squinted at her through opaque eyes. 'But not for long…'

'*Haai* Jake…'

She'd heard his rantings before. He made her feel uncomfortable. All the talk of a New South Africa, a better South Africa, a place for all its peoples, equal opportunity. She could not relate to this. Could not see a place for herself.

But Jake had hope. A vision for the future. He was politically in tune with the undercurrents, the plottings and the plannings. He'd grown up on the streets of Nyanga, had moved around in gangs, had done a stint in jail. His employer knew none of this because Jake was expedient when he had to be. Could bow and scrape with the best of them. He'd managed to hold onto this gardening job. Had been in it for eight months, which was good going for him.

Bluntly and emboldened with liquor, he stared up at her and said, 'One day I will kill this whole street. All of them. These Madams and *Mastahs* and their kids. They will all die. With my knife. With my gun. I will kill them all. Then I will walk this street and say this is my street.

This is where I mus' be. In this white house. In this white street… I will kill them all!' he shouted.

'*Haai* Jake…' Minnie watched him as she carefully edged away.

'You'll see, Minnie. One day, you'll say it happens as Jake says. Jake is right. You'll see. It will happen… We will kill them. They will die.'

She's in her room.

In her place.

In her space.

Blocked from the world.

An' never min' the politics. Never min' Jake and all his rubbish! Never min' *wat die* pastor in *die* church *se van die* equal opportunities. *Van die nuwe* South Africa. *Van die einde van* apartheid. Never min' *wat hulle se.*

It won't change for me.

This is her place.

On her own.

Not lonely.

Just alone.

The sun was high and the room was stale and sour with sweat when she woke the morning after *Tweede Nuwe Jaar*.

Minnie turned onto her back, her eyes closed. She stretched her legs, luxuriating in this time that was hers – her time, her holiday.

But the smell got to her and she threw back the bedclothes and threw her door open to a strong shaft of sunlight that cast a solid block across her bed. The dog, lying in the doorway, looked at her from the corners of his eyes. In the absence of the family, he had become as dull as the silence that surrounded him.

Barefoot and large in her nightie, Minnie stretched, yawned, scratched her head and ran her fingers through her black and grey strands of hair.

'*Kom* Blackie. *Ek gaan vir you kos en water gee.*' As she walked down the path the cracked tiles were warm under her cracked and blistered feet.

She lay in the tepid bathwater looking down at her body as though it belonged to someone else. She never had the time to do this, to look at herself as she really was. She gathered the fat on her stomach in two hands, and saw that she was fatter than she realised. Her breasts seemed bigger and there was more weight around her waist. She could feel the fat when she pinched herself. *Ag wat!* I don't care…

But it was while she was pinning her hair into its usual bun that she thought, I reely don' like these blerry pins in my head…

She thought of Madam's hair. It bounced. Madam's fringe curved over her forehead touching her eyebrows. She could flick it back with her long nails, curve a wing of smooth black hair around her ear then shake it free again.

Minnie thought that she would like to have hair like Madam's. Loose and free. Hair that moved with a toss of the head, that blew in the wind. But *Merrem*, she goes to the hairdresser every week, to that

Jono at Romanos. Cost a lot of money. A *hele klomp geld…* I wunner how much it costs? To have a haircut by that hairdresser?

A fortune! That's what Mark complained about. That *moffie* and the prices he charges!

Mus' be a lot of money. My whole wages for a month! I can never do that… Go there… Have a haircut by that Jono…

Then Minnie remembered. She sat down hard on the chair. Shaken, she realised that she could go to a place like Romano's. She had enough money to pay for a haircut at that place.

By Jono. The King. That's what the *Mastah* calls him. The King of all Hairdressers!

But —

She remembered. She was *mos* Coloured. They would never let her in.

But —

She would like Jono to cut her hair.

The top guy in the city. That's what Mark calls him. No one else in the whole world can do my wife's hair like her beloved Jono. In the whole wide world.

Only Jono. That *meshuganah* pansy in his tight black pants…

Minnie sat still and let her thoughts unfold. Maybe she could try to go there. Maybe they throw her out. But maybe she could try.

The more she thought about it the more she wanted it. She wanted her hair straightened, cut and dyed like *Merrem*'s.

She would try.

She'd take the money. Show them the money and maybe when they saw the money, the colour of her skin wouldn't matter. The money would be good enough.

She embedded it between her breasts, dabbed on eau de cologne and walked down the avenues in Granny's black sandals, excited and nervous, the sun glinting on the brass buttons of Granny's slacks suit.

The salon, red and gold and cream, near the fish and chip shop, near the station, was empty.

With palpitating heart and wet palms, she stood in the doorway and said, '*Goeie more.* Good morning.'

She answered the 'Yes?' from receptionist's small spiteful mouth. 'Excus' Miss. *Ek wil my hare… Ek… Asseblief.* I wan' to cut my *hare.*'

'You want to have your hair cut? Here?' The woman's kohl ringed eyes were fixed on the desk.

'*Ja. Ek wil dat Jono my hare sny.*'

'Jono?' The thin top lip curled up to reveal the tips of glistening enamelled teeth. 'You want Jono to cut your hair?' To herself, smiling, she said, I don't think so… Then, 'Look. There's another hairdresser around the corner. Why don't you try them? Jono's fully booked.'

'Who's fully booked?' From behind an elaborate curtain came the question. 'Daahling, I'm not fully booked. I don't have a single booking. All my daahlings are in Plett…or Tuscany…or the jungle… or some other place…'

Jonathan was thin in tight black, his face finely chiselled. He stared at Minnie, saw the dark blush in her brown cheeks. He saw her beige slack suit, her twisting hands. And said softly, 'Soo. You want a haircut… Oh, my God… Does she know what it costs?'

The receptionist shrugged her small shoulders and, perplexed, lifted her palms upwards.

'I got money.' Minnie hauled out the roll and held it towards them.

He saw the notes and said vaguely, 'Well, she can pay…' thinking not about the money, but about something else. Something long ago. Something far away… Then, laughing, he said, 'Well, for God's sake! Oh! What the hell! Honestly! Well. OK. Come along. Let's give you a haircut.'

She followed him to a cubicle at the back of the shop, her eyes staring at but not seeing his tightly swaying small backside.

'I'll do it for you. I'll cut your hair. Jono will cut your hair. Heavens alive! What's your name?'

'Minnie. *S'kuse.* Minetta. My *naam*'s Minetta.'

'Minnie. Minetta. What's the difference? You look more like a Minnie. I'll call you Minnie.' Jono had recovered. 'God. What a laugh.

Come along, Minnie. Let's get you shampooed. And let's get rid of your revolting little bun.' He poked a long finger into the centre of it. 'God, honestly! Dearest God! I don't know when I last saw anything like that! What a thing! Absolutely revolting.'

'What shall I do with the pins?' asked the shampoo girl. 'Do you want them?'

Minnie whispered '*Nee…*'

'Throw them away?' Her voice echoed through the salon.

'*Ja. Goei hulle weg…*' Minnie whispered.

Jonathan the predator move in. He lifted her stringy strands with the tail of his comb, saying, 'Heavens. It's a long time since I've seen something like this…' Then, more kindly, 'Don't worry, sweetheart. We'll fix this. We'll make you look beautiful. By the time Jono's finished with you, you'll look like a million dollars…'

He snipped and cut, moving gracefully from back to front then back again in soft leather shoes. Minnie's hair, like rats' tails, was quickly swept away by a Coloured woman who gave her a long hard look in the mirror. Minnie stared at her own reflection. The severe look was gone, the scraped-back bun had vanished. Framing her face was chopped hair that looked like a chewed mango pip.

'Don't look so shocked, angel. We're far from finished. We'll straighten it. Christine, bring Minnie some coffee while we wait for the straightener to do its wonderful work…'

Minnie froze in her seat, a magazine clutched in her hands, her coffee cold and covered with a skin of milk. She stared at the clock, stared at the minute hand. Watched the minutes tick away.

'OK, darl. This looks ready. Now we're going to put some lovely colour through it. Take out the revolting salt and pepper. I'll mix charcoal with blue. It'll look sensational! Absolutely sensational! That OK? You don't mind?'

He mixed the tubes and combed the mixture through her hair, then bound it securely with plastic wrapping. 'Half an hour, sweetheart. Read a mag. Have your coffee. I'll be back in thirty…'

She could see Jono in the mirror, his long, thin elegance. She saw him watching himself in the mirror, heard his words, his cultivated speech. She saw the dark back of his neck and, startled, thought there might be the slightest suspicion of *krill* under his sleek black hair.

Then, like the switching on of a light bulb, it came to her. My *Ghott*. Jono. *Jou skelm*! *Jy's 'n' kleurling! Fokken kleurling!* Going as white. *Haai* Jono! *Jy's mos a fokken* Coloured *moffie!*

She sat still as stone while he brushed and styled her hair, hearing him exclaim, 'Different, doll! You look absolutely, completely, indescribably, for sure – different!'

She moved her head from side to side.

'Like?' He squinted down at her.

'*Dis* different. Like you said.'

She met his gaze. They watched each other for a few moments.

'Well, that's it…' He turned away.

He knew that she knew.

It was time to pay. She peeled off the notes and walked into the street, her short chic hair shining black with a hint of midnight blue. She shook her head and felt it move.

The shampoo girl said, 'She never tipped.'

Jono watched Minnie through the window. '*Ag wat*. People like that don't tip.' His voice was gentle. 'They only put their hands out for other people to tip them.' He reached into his pocket, took out a coin and gave it to the girl.

Between buildings, light caught navy blue in the shining black short chic of her hair. Her hands kept going there, touching it, patting it down. It felt foreign, floating, as though it might blow away. The tight bun, the hairpins, all that security was gone. Now there was this free movement around her head, this deconstruction.

It made her feel unsafe.

She tried to look at her image in the Stuttafords window, to turn her head this way and that, but, instead, she saw the pink dress.

Pink.

There was not much that made Minnie excited, but she did love pink.

Pink was the one thing that gave her a sense of wonder every September in the dusty grey of her childhood. An ornamental plum tree in their barren yard, neglected and ignored, generously gave blossoms in early spring, delicate blossoms that would fall like pink snowflakes. This entrancing show only lasted a few short days.

Each year as the weather began to warm, Minnie would watch the bony branches of the naked little tree, the clusters of buds, and wait impatiently for the bursting of its beautiful blooms.

Each year on her birthday, she would have sprigs of blossoms in a glass jar next to her bed.

She stared at the dress. She saw the sweetheart neckline, the softly falling sleeves, the gathered skirt, the glowing sheen of the pink satin. It was as beautiful to her as the blossoms in spring. She wanted to touch it. To stroke the sheen.

Mus' be very expensive. In this Stuffafords. Mus' cost a lot of money.

But she remembered, with a sharp intake of breath, that she had the money.

She could pay for that dress.

She *mos* had the money.

She stood staring at the dress. Unsure. Hesitating. Her heart beating loudly.

I can buy that dress, her mind said.

I got the money.

I can get that dress for me.

Her mouth was dry and sweat beaded her broad nose. She stared at the dress and it stared back at her. They connected. She and the pink dress. The urge to try it on, to see how she looked in it, to see if it would suit her, to feel the satin against her skin, overwhelmed her.

She walked through the doors with her moving hair in Granny's old slacks suit, its brass buttons catching the lights.

Yes, the assistant knew exactly what Minnie wanted.

Yes, she did have it in her size, but really, she should try it on just to make sure.

Yes, it fitted. A little wide in the waist perhaps, but absolutely perfect over the bust.

The colour was absolutely right for her. The pink really suited her. Lovely with her dark hair. Would look lovely with silver sandals… Perfect for parties…

She held the Stuttafords bag close to her as she found her way to Ladies Shoes, to silver sandals, a silver clutch bag, pale grey pantyhose and a pink pearl on a silver chain.

They wanted to sell her lip gloss but at that Minnie baulked.

Minnie does not wear make-up. Not since her sister was caught wearing lipstick, eye shadow and pencilled eyebrows. To look older. To get the job as a machinist. But her father wasn't interested in her reasons, in her excuses. He rubbed the make-up hard over her face and then he hit her with the buckle of his leather belt. Red welts on her back and bottom were there for a long time. They turned yellow and blue.

That day, Minnie would learn that make-up was bad. Make-up was for prostitutes. Make-up was for rubbish women. Make-up was a sin and a curse.

She remembers her father's twisted face, the way his eyes grew small. She could hear the way her sister screamed. How her mother begged for him to stop. How he then hit her mother across her mouth.

The blood…

A few days later, Veronica was gone. She'd found a room with a Portuguese woman who, although not convinced, accepted her olive skin and allowed her to pretend to be white.

Veronica's manager, Ernst Bauer, was taken with her from the moment he saw her. Her sulky face, the curve of her neck, the swell of her breasts, her rounded buttocks, her smooth thighs and calves, the slimness of her ankles and the arches of her feet, all this he watched while he was watching her nimble fingers on the machine.

He thought she would be good to have sex with, but despite the flowers, the chocolates, the dinners and the wine, she resisted him.

She continued to display the cleft between her breasts. She would lick her top lip. She would stick her bottom lip out. She wore high heels. She crossed her legs and swung her foot and would let her skirt ride high on her thighs.

Her scent filled his nostrils and filtered through every part of him.

She allowed him to kiss her. She allowed him to touch her. She had a way of sitting on his lap and squirming that drove him crazy with desire for her.

But she did not allow him to have her.

He was overcome with his need for her. Thoughts of holding her naked in his bed, of exploring every part of her, of entering her deeply and roughly – these images filled his dreams and remained with him, obsessive and relentless, every day. He had to have her.

But he also found her to be soothing and empathic. She listened when he spoke, listened and heard and seemed to understand.

She ran soft hands through his hair.

She liked to sing to herself in a breathy voice.

She placed flowers in a vase one flower at a time, surveying, creating a picture, moving from one foot to another.

She curled innocently into a couch, her eyelashes forming spiked shadows on her cheeks.

She watched the stars.

He wanted her.

But he also wanted to be with her.

They married on a Wednesday and honeymooned until the Sunday. She'd just turned seventeen.


Minnie was hungry. She thought about fish 'n' chips but how would she eat it? She had too many parcels. She needed to put them down. Sit by a table. Maybe in a shop. A place where they let you sit. Like *Merrem* 'n' *Mastah*. When they 'eat out'.

Like that place where they go. The Geneva Restaurant. Down the road. Next to the pharmacy. Two blocks from where she stood thinking about food. About something to eat. The Geneva. Her Madam's favourite haunt.

She could walk past. Have a look. Not to eat. Jus' to look.

It was dim from the outside, long and narrow, and lit by small wall lamps covered in wine-coloured gold-fringed shades. Bowls of fresh roses and yellow candles stood on tables covered with immaculate white cloths.

Minnie peeped in through the door. It was empty. Too early for the dinner guests, too late for lunch.

'Can I help? Moddom?' From the plush interior, out of the rosy lighting came the well modulated accented voice of the manager.

Startled, Minnie backed out of the doorway shaking her head. '*Nee Dankie. Ek will net kyk. Dis*' a pretty place…'

'Yes, moddom. It is pretty.' His training came in useful. He did not flinch at the sight of the large coloured woman with her strange hairstyle. Instead, he almost smiled. Almost bowed.

'*Skuse Meneer.* This is a place to eat, *nê?*'

'Yes, moddom. This is the famous Geneva Restaurant.'

'But nobody is here?'

'It's too early for our dinner guests. It's also quiet at this time of the year.' He sighed. 'So many of our regulars are away.'

She was going to say, I know that. My *Merrem*'s one of your reggilers. My *Merrem*'s away. In Plett. Instead she said, 'Does this place make *vis Meneer?*'

'*Vis?*'

'*Ja. Vis.* Fish.'

'Fish. Do we make fish? Yes, indeed. We do make fish.'

'*Meneer. Kan ek n stukkie vis kry. Ek bedoel. By die tafel…*'

'I apologise, moddom. My Afrikaans is not that good. Would you mind speaking English?'

'*Jammer Meneer. Ek* is sorry. I am asking can I eat in this place. *Ek het geld…*' She hauled out the remainder of her roll of money. 'I can pay… *Ek is honger.* Hungry. An' I got a lot of parcels…'

The Frenchman did a quick mental calculation. It was highly unlikely that anyone else would come to the restaurant at this hour. She had the money. She could pay. Business was very quiet at the moment. Dead, in fact. He wrestled in his mind then decided to take the gamble. He'd let her in. She could sit at the back. In the corner.

Just in case.

'Yes, moddom. Of course. Please come in. Through here. I think moddom will like this table… Would moddom like a glass of wine? On the house of course.'

'*Wyn. Ja. Asseblief.* Please. But I can pay. I don' want for free.'

'No charge, moddom. Compliments of the house. Red or white?'

'Any one is OK. *Dankie.*'

'Now. Let's discuss your meal. You said you desire a fish dish. May I suggest our speciality – *Poisson* Hawaii. Simply delicious.'

'*Dankie. Maar ek wil net a stukkie vis hê…*'

'*Vis?* This is *kabeljou.* Caught today in Table Bay. Couldn't be fresher. Cooked in cream and white wine and fresh herbs. Simply – ' he made a kissing sound on the tips of his fingers and let them flutter above him.

'OK, *Dankie. Ek sal dit hê.* I will have it…'

On the table was her serviette folded in such a way that it had three points of equal height and width. It stood in absolute geometric perfection. Minnie was entranced. Without touching it, she tried to work out how it was constructed. She could only do one point. But before she could ask, the maître returned with a tall-stemmed glass of white wine. In one dramatic movement, he demolished the shape of the serviette as he shook it out and placed it across her lap.

'Oh, *my Ghott,*' she breathed. '*Dit* was so *mooi.*' The serviette. It was so beautiful… The way it stood…

'The serviette?'

'*Ja.* I can do one point. *Maar drie!* Three points…!'

'Would you like me to show you how to do it?'

'Oh. *Ja. Asseblief.* Please. Will you?'

'Yes. Of course I'll show you.' He whipped the serviette from another table, and with much flourishing, demonstrated how and where to fold. Three perfect points.

'*Dis baie mooi,*' Minnie whispered. 'My *Merrem* will reely like that…'

The maître gave no indication of what he'd just heard. He showed her again, then repeated the method one more time. 'You try now,' he said in a gentle voice.

Minnie tried. She folded and pulled. There it was, the three-pointed standing serviette.

She smiled at him. Her eyes were soft and warm. '*Baie baie dankie Meneer*. Thank you so very much. *Dis* so beautiful. I will never forget what you show me.'

Mark's father Sam was a self-made man. Came from nothing. Grew up in Fordsburg. Went to Jewish Government School. Started work at thirteen.

'Mind you,' he would generously concede, 'I wasn't the only one. There were plenty poor Jews in Fordsburg. Plenty.'

He told the children that he delivered newspapers, 'Early morning run. I started at five in the morning. Pitch dark. Icy cold. That's how it was.' His eyes screwed up. 'Not spoilt like you kids of today. We grew up tough. Bladdy tough. Never did us any harm, though. Look at me. I came through it. Made a big success. Came through the hard times. Worked hard. Bladdy hard. Teaches you something to grow up tough. Teaches you to survive. To see things through. Never to give up. Doesn' do you any harm to grow up tough.'

They like his story about Black Jack Chewing Gum. 'First chewing gum this country's ever seen. We got a job promoting it. Me an' the Berlinsky twins – Solly, an' I forget the name of the other one. Mus' be getting old… Fancy me forgetting the other twin's name…'

They'd stood in the OK Bazaars window and chewed the gum and blown bubbles for the crowd who then bought the liquorice gum four pieces for a penny.

'I can tell you, our jaws were bladdy sore by the time we'd done our shift an' we was covered in it, all over our faces, our eyebrows, our hair. But we sold that gum. We earned our few pennies an' we was happy!' His face beamed and creased with joy.

For those who would listen, Sam would continue. 'I grew into a strong boy. Anyone got bullied, anyone called a bladdy Jew, they'd call me. Sam, they'd say, that's the one. Boy, I'd land him one! One punch to the jaw and he saw stars… So then I got a job loading and unloading furniture onto trucks for a large warehouse. I could carry a two-seater couch on my own up three flights of stairs. I was only fifteen but they thought I was eighteen.

That's what I told 'em. They was happy with me. Gave me a rise each year and a Christmas bonus. I was there seven years. They thought they had me for life. But I was too clever for that. Never had much schooling but I had *seichel* – I was aware, clever, one step ahead.' His finger tapped his forehead. 'That counts for a lot. Always told my boy *seichel* counts for more than academics. *Seichel* is what gets you there.'

The company were all the time congratulating themselves on what a hard-working industrious boy they had in Sam.

He was all the time watching and waiting, getting to know the factories that made the furniture, learning the costs of buying, the profits of selling, and building relationships with the owners.

He learned the values of the different woods and how to value the workmanship. With his sharp eyes and hungry mind, he internalised all aspects of the furniture market.

'They thought I was a workhorse idiot. But all the time I was watchin' an' waitin'. Waitin' for my turn. My time to make a buck. Not jus' a buck. Big bucks.'

He opened his first shop in Doornfontein. Dining room tables and sideboards lined the long narrow badly lit space. Chairs hung from the ceiling. Outside the shop and in the window one chair from each suite was displayed to tempt the shoppers.

The prices were always inflated to allow for negotiations and the buyer always left satisfied that he'd bought a bargain. Sam did the deliveries himself after hours and visited the factories at seven in the morning. He looked after his accounts, checking and rechecking to see that he hadn't been cheated.

Sam worked fourteen hours a day, six days a week. He paid off his bank loan. He took a bond on a small house in Yeoville. He bought a second-hand Studebaker.

He opened a bigger store in the middle of the city. Then another a few street away.

In the ten years that followed, he established three large furniture stores and had shares in two furniture manufacturing companies.

In a pure wool suit, an imported shirt, a silk tie and black leather shoes, Sam was now firmly on his way.

He met Carmel at a dance in the synagogue hall. She was a small dark-haired girl with large brown eyes and high colour in her cheeks. She liked him immediately, his large frame, his big head, his thick brown hair that stood up at the crown no matter how hard he brushed it, his contagious grin and, mostly, his air of confidence and self-assurance.

They came together like two halves of a whole. They built a mansion with a sweeping staircase. There were servants, chauffeured cars, a large circle of wealthy friends. It should have been idyllic.

But Sam had a weakness. He loved women. He loved the curves of their cheeks, the glossiness of their coiffed hair. He loved their soft hands where diamonds nestled and the play of diamonds on their wrists. He loved their perfumes, the clefts between their breasts, the suggestion in their wide or sleepy eyes, their rounded backsides, their rounded thighs, their calves and ankles and down to their toes. He watched their smiles, the glint on their wet teeth, the fullness of their lips. He was drawn to their mouths like a moth to a candle flame.

Carmel had to watch him. She was so practised that she could spot the woman he would be making a beeline for before he made his moves. She was never sure how far his dalliances went, choosing in her own mind to play them down.

But sometimes in the privacy of their bedroom she would let him have it, shouting, How could he? So insensitive! So disrespectful! Did he not realise that they were all watching him? That they laughed behind his back! That they felt pity for her!

She berated him.

He shouted back.

She cried.

He said she was talking nonsense. She was imagining things…

She threw a shoe at him…

But their arguments remained just that.

She was his wife. At all times she was his wife, and that's who she would always be. She'd supported him in building his fortune. She'd raised their son with love and dedication. She'd played her role of gracious hostess in their immaculately run home. Never would she allow her position to be usurped.

Despite his wandering eye, Sam really did love her. He relied on her more than she would ever know. She was always there. She listened, she advised, she empathised. Her presence calmed and reassured him.

He would tell anyone who listened that he had the best wife in the world. The best. That he loved her with every fibre of his being. That, if he had it all over, he would, without any doubt, marry her all over again.

But he still had an eye for the women. That's how it was.


They'd struggled to have a child. Carmel had three miscarriages. Her fourth pregnancy confined her mainly to her bed.

She leaned against her pillows day after day for most of the nine months filled with trepidation. At the slightest twinge, she would lie like a stone with clenched fists and tears running down her face.

With all her might, she willed that the tiny life within her would survive.

Early in her ninth month, she give birth to a small red-faced boy with spiky black hair.

Carmel took him to her breast immediately. Overcome with love for the child, she meticulously set about being the best mother she could – feeding, bathing and changing the child herself, crooning to him, cuddling him, forever watching his little face, his dark eyes, his pink cheeks. Forever telling him how much she loved him.

She smiled at him, laughed when he chuckled, showed him picture books, gave him toys. Ignored all warnings of spoiling him. Indulged him, and indulged herself in caring for him.


Mark was a clever precocious child who charmed everyone with his handsome dark looks and cheeky smile. He knew how to captivate his audience and always took for granted that he would be the centre of attraction.

There was a nanny in an antiseptic white uniform who stood at attention, ready to fetch a biscuit or a wet cloth to wipe his hands. To pick up after him. To clean his mess. She was not charmed by the child. He treated her with disdain. She, in turn, never lost an opportunity to glare at him from behind his mother's back, or to give him a push or a pinch on the rare occasions that she had him on his own.

Mark was handsome and successful. He was clever and athletic. He should have been head boy of the school. That's what his parents expected. But he was not liked and the students voted for another boy.

Sam secretly made an appointment to see the headmaster. Sam was on the school board. He'd made significant donations to the school.

Mark's the cleverest, brightest and most talented boy amongst them all. He deserves to be head boy. All this he told the headmaster.

It fell on deaf ears.

Mark said, 'Who cares? I'm better than all of them.'

He graduated with the highest marks in all subjects in his year.


Sitting in the lecture room in the commerce faculty, he noticed a slim, sleek-haired girl with long legs and long milky hands, her pointed chin, her finely chiselled nose, the fall of her dark hair that she constantly pushed behind her ears.

She sat in rapt attention, taking notes, her legs crossed, one foot restlessly moving up and down. At the end of the lecture, she would gather her papers and slip gracefully from the room. Her name was Dana Silver. A Jewish girl from a respectable family.

She was clever. Every bit as clever as him. She had a quiet presence. She was careful in all that she said and did.

He was captivated by her dark mysterious eyes. By her shy smile.

One of his friends said that she had mystique.

He liked that description of her. Intriguing. Somewhat unfathomable. Someone he needed to get to know.

They were engaged a month after they graduated. It was a party celebrated in grand style in his parents' mansion.

The girl, tall and slender, was elegant in silver, her hair as sleek and exquisite as the wings of a raven. She wore no jewellery except for a massive diamond engagement ring on the third finger of her left hand.

'She's made a good *shiddach* – a good match,' they said at the wedding. A very good *shiddach* – at least in terms of wealth.

In an atmosphere of celebration and congratulations, of smiling approval and nodding heads, one man had silent misgivings.

Dana's father, a quiet introspective man, adored his daughter. He'd hoped that she would have known more of the world before jumping into marriage. He recognised that Mark was young, the same age as Dana.

Indulged. Self-centred. With attitude.

But, he told himself, they were in love.

He sat smiling at the main table staring at the glorious fruit and flower decorations and determinedly pushed aside his uneasiness and the dislike he had for his new son-in-law.


His wife, on the other hand, could not take to Maralyn.

The girl had practically grown up in their house. From a fuzzy-haired child to a precocious teenager, and now a beautiful and sexy young woman, Maralyn had known how to make Dana laugh, taught her how to dance, showed her how to wet her lips with her tongue, how to quizzically raise one eyebrow. They were best friends.

Dana was Maralyn's maid of honour at her wedding. Maralyn, with her telltale bump, was matron of honour for Dana.

Amazing, Dana's mother told her husband, how Maralyn still managed to swing her backside with being pregnant and everything.

He winked back at her. 'That's Maralyn,' he grinned.

That's when she realised what it was that she didn't like about her. It was her twitching backside.

Plettenberg Bay is a pretty place. From Mark and Dana's rented house can be seen the curve of the beach and a line that stretches across the horizon that divides sea and sky. It is a blue and white space only interrupted by flocks of birds or the silver dot of a distant plane. It's a place where one can find one's peace.

But Mark was not looking for peace. He was high on desire, strung out like a teenager awakened to the first stirrings of sex. He woke each day with only one thing on his mind – how to get Maralyn on his own. It did not matter where – in the waves, on the dance floor – wherever and whenever. And, he knew, she was up for it. Giving out signals in the way her hips moved, the bulge of her breasts from the sides of her bikini top, her pointed nipples when she came wet from the sea.

Her husband Dave stretched out in his beach chair, his nose in his newspaper. Behind his rimless reading glasses, he studied the stock market. Jokes were made that Dave was married to his newspaper. But that was not so. Dave was married to Maralyn and no one knew that better than Dave. She was his first and only love, a schoolgirl when they started dating, his beautiful young bride and devoted mother to his children.

Dave, behind his glasses, immersed in his paper, was aware of what was going on. He saw almost everything, and what he did not see he absorbed through his pores. His wife's little adventures, as he privately referred to them, never bothered him. Mark was not the first. He would not be the last. Dave recognised that men would always be drawn to Maralyn and that she would be open to their advances – her smoothness and creaminess, her plumpness and her slenderness, her slow smile and her thickly fringed violet eyes, her tinges of rose, her lovely tinges of peach…

He also knew that she loved him. That he was first in her life. He knew that her diversions had no significance. She would walk away from them without a backward glance. So Dave studied the stock market, quietly amassed his fortune, and spoiled and indulged his adored wife's every whim. He managed his life by appearing uncommunicative, grunting when spoken to, seemingly vague, somewhat distant. It was his way of keeping control.

Dana was not in control. Lying on her towel, sharply angled and bony, she stared unseeing at the sea through large dark glasses. She and Maralyn had always been best friends. Had always shared their innermost thoughts and feelings. But in recent months Dana had felt uneasy when the four of them were together. She blamed Mark, knowing him to have what his father had jokingly described as a roving eye.

'Don't worry about him.' He'd grinned at Dana. 'Mark only looks. Nothing else. Like all men,' he winked. 'We all look. That's how men are...'

But this was different. It was as though Mark was not there, not with her, nor with the children. He spent more time in the bathroom each morning, walked with a spring in his step, laughed too much, and smiled all the time.

He'd never seemed happier. But his happiness did not flow to her or for her. His happiness was for himself.

Maralyn was also different. As always, she was loving and responsive, but she too was extraordinarily active, bouncing up to swim whenever Mark said, 'Anyone ready to go in?' looking at Maralyn as though the question was meant for her.

When Jarryd replied, 'I'll go in with you, Dad!' he smiled and said, 'Later, Jarryd. Later...' and ran into the waves with Maralyn, her shoulder brushing his arm.

They came out of the water wet and laughing and fetched coffee from the cafeteria. As they walked off, Dana noticed that Mark was pressed against up Maralyn and that his hand was lightly on her bare hip. She saw them turn to each other, and exchange brief smiles.

'I'll go with you,' Dana said.

But they walked ahead of her, his head bent towards Maralyn's blonde curls, unaware that she was behind them until they got to the kiosk.

Mark turned round, saw her, then brusquely asked, 'What are you doing here?'

Her reply, 'I've come to help with carrying the cups,' sounded inane.

He shrugged and turned away.

The next morning, they were stretched out on the sand. Mark asked, 'Who wants oil?'

'I'll have some.' He rubbed it over Dana's shoulders and back.

'And me…' came Maralyn's soft response.

Mark knelt next to Maralyn's barely clad body. He poured oil into his cupped hand and spread it over her bare shoulders. She pulled her bikini straps away. He moved his hands down her arms. She lay on her forearms, her face turned towards him. He stroked oil over her back in slow caressing movements, lightly touched the sides of her breasts that bulged from her bikini, and moved down her back and the sides of her body, towards the crease of her bottom.

Dana sat up on her towel. Mark was rubbing oil on the backs of Maralyn's thighs. She saw Maralyn moving her thighs apart. She saw Mark's hand between her thighs.

Dana glanced quickly at Dave but as always he was hidden behind his reading glasses, behind his newspaper, open on the page for stock markets.

She felt bile rise from her stomach. She was watching a scene between her husband and her best friend that was deeply distressing to her, something sexual, intimate, confronting.

She stood up and said abruptly, 'OK, Mark. That's enough! I think Maralyn's got enough oil on her to last her for a week.'

Maralyn glanced at her friend's tight unsmiling lips, the stony expression on her face. She said nothing. She turned her face away and closed her eyes.

In the late afternoon, Mark put on his running shoes. She watched him run up the street and disappear over the hill.

She made herself a cup of tea and told the boys to have a bath. It was getting late. They needed to have their supper. It was nearly time for bed.

She decided to phone Maralyn. To ask her what she was going to wear that evening. To ask whether she should wear the black dress or the white slacks suit with the silver beading.

Dave answered. He sounded as though he'd been sleeping. 'Maralyn?' He yawned. 'She's not here.'

'Oh? Where is she?'

'She's gone for a run. With Mark.' He yawned. 'Sorry, Dana. I've just woken up.'


Dana walked into the Blue Flamingo with Mark. She knew at once that she should not have worn the beaded slacks suit. It was too formal.

In contrast, Maralyn looked like a young girl in a long slip of pink silk, her hair a cascade of blonde curls, her skin bronzed, her eyes violet and sparkling, and just a hint of lustrous lipstick on her sultry lips.

Dave had arrived having downed two whiskies. He promptly had two more in rapid succession. Then after a hazy turn around the floor, he sank into a seat in a corner and said to Mark, 'I'm drunk. You'll have to dance with my wife this evening.'

Mark took Maralyn in his arms as though she belonged there. She melted into him as he moved her away from their table. They were soon lost in the crowd and the dim lighting.

One song followed another. Dana sat and waited for them. She tried to find them in the dancing throng but she could not see them.

She got up and walked around the dance floor.

They were on the other side of the floor. His arms were around her, his hand on her bottom, his lips on her forehead. She held him, her fingers in his hair. Her head nuzzled into his neck. They looked at each other, smiling deeply into each other's eyes. Their lips touched. He leaned over her. She folded into his embrace.

They wanted each other. Dana could see that. If they were away from the crowd, they would have taken each other with ferocious need, with overwhelming passion.

She stared at them. Mark and Maralyn. Oh, God. Her husband… Her best friend…

Dana's chest tightened. Her heart began to beat louder, faster. Her head pounded. The room went dark. She could not breathe.

She turned away and, holding onto the backs of chairs, returned to their table.

Dave was lying back in his seat. His eyes were closed. He seemed asleep. In his hand a glass leaned, its contents close to being tipped out.

She glanced at him.

He opened his eyes.

'Hi,' he said. 'You OK?' Then closed them again.

Her face was drained, her body shaking. She picked up her white beaded evening bag and numbly walked out of the room.

The sun was high and the day hot. A fly flew around the small closed room. It settled on Minnie's nose. In her sleep, she brushed it away.

Outside, a buzz of insects, and the winey smell of crushed plums, and the whine of the dog at her door.

She was not sure whether she was woken by Granny knocking on her door, or whether she was already awake when she heard the knocks. She opened her eyes each morning and, out of habit, resolved to get up. Then, remembering with pleasure that she was on holiday, dozed again in the warmth of the drowsy mornings.

In her voluminous nightie and *doek*, her feet square and bare, she stood and blinked against the sun.

The crumpled face of Granny was outlined in the glare. 'Sorry, Minnie. Sorry to wake you.'

'It's OK, Granny.' Minnie scratched.

'Look. I'm really sorry to disturb you. I know it's your holiday. I wouldn't have disturbed you but I got a call from Dana, from Madam this morning, she phoned from Plett, they're coming home today, her and the children. They're cutting the holiday short, they're flying back today, leaving at half past eleven, they'll be back this afternoon, she's very upset, very upset...' These words from Granny's anguished lips.

'Today, Granny?' Minnie played for time, her senses alert.

'Yes. Today. This afternoon. They'll be back this afternoon. I know it's your holiday, and I really don't want to disturb you, but Madam said can you open up the windows and dust and make the beds and that we should make supper for the kids... They'll pay you for this, Minnie. They'll pay you for this time...'

'It's OK, Granny. I'll jus' wash and get dress' an' I'll come. Don' worry. I'll come now. I'll make quick.'

Minnie stared at her image in the bathroom mirror then sat down hard on the toilet seat before standing up again. Her short dyed hair shocked her. I'll have to wear a *doek,* she said, fingering the blue-black wisps.

Yesterday's activities came back in a flood of confused thought. The hair. The dress. The other stuff. With a sudden and terrible sense of loss, she thought about the money.

All that money.

Gone.

*Agh, wat!* she sighed, *dis mos net geld.* To tell the *troot, ek is mos bly dis weg. Daaie geld* was too much worry for me.


The house was large in its emptiness. The curtains had shut out light and shut in the stale air.

Granny, her hair grey and lifeless, her face creased, hunched over the telephone and leaned her cheek into her hand. She drew intensely on a cigarette, removed something from the tip of her tongue, and said to her sister, 'I don't know what she's going to do. I'm telling you, Ethel, this could be the end. I'm not joking. This could be the break-up. She sounds terrible. Crying hysterically in front of the children. What? I know it's not good for the kids. I could hear Jeremy shouting in the background. Oh, he was saying he doesn't want to come back. And Mark was yelling if the kids don't want to leave, they can stay with him. It's just too terrible.

'What? Well, she's convinced he's having an affair with Maralyn. She says she knows. She's absolutely convinced there's something going on between them. She says that the entire holiday all they've done is give each other the eye. She told me every time he goes into the water to swim, that little bitch follows him and they swim together for hours. And last night, well, she says that took the cake. He danced with her like they were sleeping together.

'What? I don't know. She didn't say. Just said that like they were sleeping together. I suppose very intimate, you know, very close. I don't know. That's what she said. The husband? I don't know. I asked Dana if he's upset, and she says she doesn't know. She says he takes no notice. Just reads the stock exchange reports. She says that's all he does all day long – reads the stock exchange reports.

'What? I did ask her. I said why doesn't she say anything to Maralyn. She said she did, already a few days ago.

'What? Oh, she said, "What's up with you and Mark?"

'What? Oh, she laughed it off. Said it was all Dana's imagination. Said, "For God's sake, Dana, we're all good friends" and "This is a holiday. Just chill out and try and enjoy yourself." Ever heard that in your life? Little bitch. Good friends! What does she think? My daughter's a fool? God, Ethel, you know Dana. She's no fool. If she says something's going on, she knows. She doesn't manufacture things.

'Anyway, she's very, very upset and she and the kids are coming home this afternoon. I'm telling you, Ethel, this could be the end of their marriage. He's got an eye for the women, we've always known that. But this time it's been too much for Dana. Poor girl. She's so upset. She's beside herself.'

Granny lit another cigarette with the end of the first one, inhaled deeply and coughed. 'God, Ethel… If Dana was here now, she'd kill me. I swore to her that I've stopped smoking. Now I'm smoking like a bladdy chimney. I'm so aggravated…

'Oh, here's Minnie. Thank God for her. Minnie, please be a darling and bring me a cup of coffee – very little milk. Thanks.

'Oh, Ethel. What are we going to do? I'm devastated for her, for the kids. It's terrible, just terrible… I'm not counting my chickens before they hatch. I know my daughter. When she's like this, she could do it.

'What? Divorce. That's what I'm talking about… Divorce! Oh, my God… The kids. What about the poor kids…

'Thanks, Minnie. I'm dying for that. Haven't had a thing today, not to drink, not to eat. I'm beside myself.

'What? Ethel, I couldn't swallow a crumb, never mind a piece of toast. I'd choke. That's how I feel. I'd absolutely choke.'

Minnie drew back the heavy silk curtains in the lounge and opened the glass doors to the lawns, the plane trees and the rose garden. The day glowed in greens and blues. The air was gentle, the flagstones warm.

On the terrace, the wrought-iron chairs were bare.

She gave the furniture in the lounge a cursory dusting, the butler's table, the teapoy, the credenza, names that rolled off Dana's tongue, the bergère chair deeply buttoned and upholstered in green silk, antiques that *Merrem* mixed so well with her moderns.

They all said that. Dana really knows how to mix antiques with modern.

'Her lounge looks amazing!'

'And her paintings! She really has an eye for art.'

'Ask Dana to come with you when you buy. She's so good when it comes to putting stuff together.'

The room with its lofty ceiling, its pale walls.

Persian rugs in rich silks of ruby and sapphire, cream wool settees and rich side tables, all grouped around a marble coffee table displaying a magnificent bronze sculpture of a man and a horse.

The ornaments. The long thin pieces together, the rounded and oblongs mixed, the rosewoods shot through in gold and amber, glowing in golden light.

Then the dining room with its huge table and Hepplewhite chairs, shield-backed, with fluted legs. Silver candlesticks and serving dishes.

The priceless chandelier that Mark's mother said cost an arm and a leg.

She'd heard the fights her Madam and Master had about his *skollie* ways. About what the hell's going on with him? About the other women he's always ogling. About the women he sidles up to and puts his arms around. About who the fuck does he think he is! Casanova?

*Hulle was net soos die* Coloured *mense, net met geld.* They're just the same as Coloured people, except for money.

*Maar*, she conceded, *hy slaan haar nie. Hy skree en hy blaspheme – en ook haar. Maar hy use nie sy fists nie.* He doesn't hit her. He screams and she screams, but he doesn't use his fists.

All this stuff, all this antique, thought Minnie, wiping the shield-backed chairs, their fluted legs. Doesn't help.

They have the money. They have this stuff.

But it doesn't help. Their troubles are just the same as ours.

Mark opened the front door ahead of the two boys. He threw a suitcase to the floor and shouted for Minnie.

Dana's mother nervously curved into herself against the wall.

'What are you doing here?' His voice flat, his eyes flattened.

'Hello, Mark.' She tried to smile. 'I've been staying here with Dana.'

'You've been staying with Dana?'

'Yes.'

'How long have you been here?'

'Since she came back. I've been keeping her company.'

'So… You've been keeping my lovely wife company, have you?'

'I have…' She tried to smile. Her smile was broken.

'Well, I'm back now, so you can leave.'

'What?'

'I said I'm back, so you can leave. Now.'

'Oh. OK. I'll just get my things…' She shrank backwards towards the staircase, gripping the bannister until her knuckles bulged. 'I'll get my things… Say goodbye to Dana… She's upstairs…'

His back was turned to her. 'Well, make it snappy. I want you gone by the time I've brought the luggage in… Where's Minnie?'

'*Mastah?*' Minnie was in the shadow of the passage. Her face was bland. She had long learned to shut down when there was a punishing rush in the air, a bristling of the airwaves.

Dana leaned over the bannister. Her hair fell forward. 'Are they back? The kids? Are they back?' She flew down the stairs, her arms wide to catch them, to feel their bony bodies against her, to look into the shining bronze of their faces, to rub her hands through the shining dark of their hair, to smell the sun's rays.

'You've grown. I think you've grown.'

They heard the catch in her voice. Their arms were tight around her.

'Are you crazy?' Mark cut in. 'How could they have grown in ten days?'

'They seem taller. I think they seem taller.' Her voice faltered.

'They're just the same as they were. Your eyes are deceiving you.'

They stood, the three women, transfixed by him, by the set expression in his eyes, by words that squeezed from the corner of his mouth, by the mean line of his lips. He dropped the suitcases and instructed Minnie to unpack. He glanced coldly and meaningfully at Dana's mother who scurried away to collect her things.

The boys ran after Minnie.

They were left to face each other. 'You look like shit,' he said quietly.

'I've been very upset…'

'You've been upset. You bugger up a holiday. You leave in the middle. You desert your children…'

'What! What are you saying? I did not desert the kids! I wanted to take them with me! You said no! You wouldn't allow them to come home with me!'

'Well, why should they cut their holiday short? They were having a great time. Everyone was having a great time. Except you. You chose to bugger off. Packed your bags and were gone! The others couldn't believe what you did. To your own kids…'

'What are you talking about? We had this conversation and you flatly refused to let them come with me. I couldn't stay there any more. I couldn't stand it. I wanted to take them…'

'Well, all I can tell you is that the place was buzzing with what you did. They all thought it was disgusting leaving me on my own to look after the boys. People were asking what kind of a mother you are, what kind of mother does that.'

'So you're blaming me? Is that what you're doing? You behave like an animal, and you blame me! How do you mean, the place was buzzing? What did you tell them? Did you tell them what was going on with you and Maralyn? Did you tell them that!'

Mark's face froze. He took a step forward. His eyes burned. Anger was in every part of him, in his face, his shoulders, his fists. 'What did you say?' His voice was quiet, venomous.

'I said did you tell them about Maralyn and you?'

He raised his fist. 'What about Maralyn and me?' His face was in front of hers. 'Tell me. What? What do you know? What did you see?'

'I know what I saw. I saw the two of you carrying on…'

'You saw us carrying on! Me and your best friend? You saw us carrying on. You're crazy, you know. You're absolutely crazy…'

'Don't call me crazy!' she shouted. 'Don't you call me crazy.' She flew at him, pummelled him with her fists and screamed, 'Don't you dare call me crazy…'

He grabbed her wrists. Held her away from him and pushed her backwards.

She fell against the stairs and screamed, 'I know what was going on between the two of you. I know what I saw…' She held her head in her hands, her hair fell like a curtain over her face. She sobbed.

'You know what you saw?' His face was ugly. 'What you saw was in your head, in your twisted jealous mind…' And then quietly, menacingly, 'You've lost it, you know. Completely lost it. You've lost your mind. You need to see a psychiatrist. Urgently…'

Dana's mother trudged lopsided into her flat pulling, pushing, her bag. Her face was crumpled and grey and darkly smudged beneath her creased eyes. The bag clattered to the floor and she stood unsteady, reaching for the back of an armchair.

Her husband looked up from the dining room table and said, surprised, 'Oh, you're back.'

The good smell of warm toast came to her.

'Yes. He's back. He chucked me out…'

'Who? Mark?'

'Yes. He's back. He threw me out of the house…'

'How do you mean?'

'I'm telling you. He chucked me out. He came home in a terrible mood…'

'Was Dana there?'

'Of course she was there. You know, she hasn't left the house since she got back. I heard them having a helluva go at each other. I slipped out when he went to the kitchen. Never even had a chance to say goodbye to her.'

'Well, of course they'd have a go at each other. Stands to reason. She left in the middle of the holiday. He would come back mad as all hell.'

'What about her? She had good reason to leave.'

'Did she? I don't know. I mean, did she actually catch them together in what they call a compromising situation? You know what I mean. Having sex. She didn't. They were probably having a harmless flirtation. That's how some young people are. And we know that Mark's always had an eye for the women. Doesn't mean he did something…'

'I believe her. I know my daughter. She wouldn't make things up. If she thought they were sleeping together, then ninety-nine per cent she's right. She's a clever sensible girl. She wouldn't make up things in her mind.'

'And I know Mark. I can't imagine he would gamble his marriage by going the whole hog. Sure, he must have given her some reason to react like she did, but, as I say, nothing serious.'

Dana's mother twisted her rings. She turned round to find Sue-Ellen at the door. 'My God. How long have you been standing there?'

'*Nee Merrem*. I was jus' in the bedroom. Would *Merrem* like some tea?'

'Yes. Please. And Sue…please unpack my things. There's some washing in the bag… I s'pose she heard the whole conversation…'

'Doubt it. She was in the bedroom. But to come back to Dana… The best thing she could do is to forget about it. Make up with Mark, and make up with Maralyn. I mean, for God's sake, Maralyn's her best friend…'

'You try telling her that. She can't stand talking about her. And when she does, she only has bad things to say. I can't see that friendship ever coming right.'

'More important, she needs to make her marriage right. She doesn't want a divorce on her hands. They've got two boys to bring up.' He chewed his toast then fixed his gaze firmly on her. 'You're her mother. You better tell her what I'm saying. Put the whole thing to bed once and for all. Forget it. Make up with Mark and get back to living a life.'

Granny was in turmoil. She thought, I know that Dana's a sensible girl. She doesn't imagine things. If she thinks she saw something, even if she didn't actually see it, usually she's right. In her heart, she knew that Dana was right.

She'd watched Maralyn, had seen her eyes become sleepy when she looked at Mark, saw her slow smile. She'd never liked her, even as a child. Had hoped that Dana would break the friendship.

'Why would I, Mom?' was Dana's response. 'She's a good friend. Very kind. Very generous. She's good for me. She's outgoing. She's the one who gets invited to everything. She helps me along. Wants me to be with her. She's fun. Good for a laugh. And we're very close. We tell each other everything. We actually get on like sisters.'

Now her best friend, her almost-sister, had betrayed her. Mark had betrayed her.

She told her mother that she would not stay in the marriage. 'You don't understand!' she'd shout. 'I don't want him! I don't trust him! I can't look at him!'

'But don't you still have feelings for him? You were so much in love?'

'Love him? I don't love him. I hate him! I hate the sight of him!'

Dana's mother listened and nodded. She could not argue against Dana. But, she told herself, time would heal.

'Wait. Give it time,' she told her husband, trying to quell her own anxiety. 'Time's a great healer.'

Jack did not believe in waiting. He said to Dana, 'For God's sake, put it behind you. Forget it. Put it to bed. Get on with your life. What do you want? A divorce? Remember, you've got two kids. Two boys. They need a father and a mother. Think of them. They're the ones who'll suffer. Is that what you want? For your two boys to suffer? Even if Mark had a little flirtation, don't attach so much importance to it.

For God's sake! It's not the end of the world. You're his wife. Remember that. You're the one he married.' He told her to think of Jeremy and Jarryd.

Two small boys. Confused and frightened. Their mom and dad, two people who loved them and looked after them, were now fighting and shouting and banging doors on each other. They were no longer caring for them. They seemed not to see them, or hear them, or hold them. Granny was there, and Grandpa, and the other grandparents. They were doing everything for them.

But the boys didn't want the grannies and grandpas. They wanted their mom and dad.

Minnie checked that they'd brushed their teeth. She looked behind their ears.

She seemed to be there for whatever they needed, silent but constant, with a different expression in her eyes, a kindness they'd not seen before.

'Is Mom sick?' they asked.

'Maybe,' she said.

'Will she get better?'

'Maybe she will…'

'Dad said that Mom's made herself sick…'

Minnie was silent.

'Dad said she's got funny ideas in her head. That's what's making her sick…'

'Dad said she put these funny ideas in her head by herself. She made herself sick.'

Jeremy threw himself on the floor. He banged his hands and kicked his feet. 'I hate her!' he screamed. 'She doesn't talk! She doesn't do anything… She just locks the door… Won't let me in…'

Jarryd cried and threw himself against her apron, his arms around her large waist. He hung onto her, his head buried into her side. 'She doesn't get dressed. She doesn't help me with my homework. She doesn't fetch us from school. She's causing all this trouble. It's all her fault!'

'*Haai* Jarryd. Don' cry.' She wiped his tears with a tissue. 'Come. You mus' get ready. The lift is coming…'

Mark did not care. That was his attitude to most things. You fitted in with him, or fell out with him. That was his motto in life. I'm easy going, he liked to say. BUT – don't cross my path. Don't push me. Don't push my buttons. He was always right. Even when he did the wrong thing, behaved in the wrong way, he never saw his actions to be anything other than fun, a joke, harmless.

He was a guy who loved life. Sure, he lived a little on the edge, but what the hell? He was young and full of fight. He was going to give it all he had. You're only young once, for God's sake! All this fuss about such *kuck*! Mark could swear. He could give it stick! If you made him angry, he'd use every four-letter word in one sentence without repeating any of them.

When he was angry, he got white around the mouth. His eyes became pinpricks, his nose seemed sharp. He'd smash a vase. He'd throw a shoe at you. He'd kick a chair across the room. He clenched his fists and punched the air. He'd show you his fist. In your face.

Funny thing, he hardly ever shouted. He spoke in a small mean tone out of the corner of his mouth. Said mean and nasty things that made you sorry you went there. He could make mincemeat of you with his cutting tongue, with his insults and threats. Then, when you cringed, he would smile, and his smile was cold and cruel – was more threatening than his curled upper lip.

Or he retreated into silence. No communication. No eye contact. That was worse than his anger, much more difficult to live with, and could go on for two or three weeks. Come in, go out, eat, sleep, but not speak. Stare out of the window. Stare at the TV.

All this, Dana had experienced. She kept it to herself, mostly blaming herself. She should not have… Why did she…? How stupid she was to have… She should have known…

He called her ugly. Skinny. Said she had no bum, no tits, no sex appeal. She tried to eat more, to put on weight. But as soon as her jeans became tight, she stopped eating. Her jeans were her monitor. They kept her thin. She could not not fit into her jeans.

She began to see herself as unattractive. Undesirable.

She spent vast sums of money on her hair, on beauty treatments, on massages, and spent hours working in the gym. She bought expensive clothing, shoes, jewellery. She bought imported handbags, designer scarves. She did everything she could to make herself feel better.

But the effects were short-lasting. Small injections that lifted her spirits for a while before her terrible feelings of inadequacy returned. Even the hours spent on the phone to her friends, the gossip, the latest traumas in the lives of others, only made her feel better until the call had ended and she was left to face her own struggles, her pain, the difficulties of her life.

In her way, she pushed through each day and appeared to manage. She saw to the house and the children. She entertained their friends and they returned the visits.

Generally speaking, they seemed an OK kind of couple, although those who knew the other side of Mark always said Dana deserved a medal. You have to be some tough lady to live with him, they muttered. God knows how she does it…

But the latest episode was too much. Her husband and her best friend. Absolutely devastating. Enough to push anyone over the edge. Teetering on the edge of a precipice. On her knees. Hanging on by her fingernails. She was clutching at straws.

Mark saw.

He knew.

He did not care.

The house became a shadow of its previous life.

There had been one Shabbat since Mark's return, a feeble attempt to reclaim what was no longer there.

The grandparents came. Dave and the children came. Maralyn stayed away.

'She's got a migraine,' Dave said. That was all he said.

Dana's mother did the shopping and helped to prepare the food. They worked side by side in the kitchen. Chopping, slicing, stirring, tasting.

'You know, Minnie. I'm very upset what's happened with Madam and Master.'

'*Ja* Granny…'

'I don't know what to do…'

Minnie threw the carrots into the stew. 'Is bad, Granny…'

'It is bad. Bad for them and bad for the kids…'

'*Ja* Granny…'

'I wish Madam would put this all behind her. You know, just forget about it and make peace again. Make up with Mark and let their lives get back to normal. It's terrible for everyone. We're all so upset with this whole business. I worry for her and I worry for the kids…'

Minnie carried on stirring. Harsh feelings stirred inside her. Granny is not right. She jus' want them to make it right for other people to feel better. She want *Merrem* to *sommer so forgit* what happen. Is not so easy. You don' forgit. Is very hard. Something happen inside you. Like a big stone. Inside you all the time…

She said, '*Ja* Granny.'

They want Dana to resume her life, light the Shabbat candles, say the *brocha*, smile and be warm and welcoming. They want to believe that she over-reacted. Had taken it too far. That she'd created chaos in her home. That she'd upset her family and her friends. They're questioning whether Mark and Maralyn had actually done anything wrong to warrant such upset. They're beginning to think that perhaps there is something wrong with Dana.

Dana knew that they were doubting her. No one seemed to be on her side. 'Maybe I am going crazy?' she thought.

But there was one person who believed her, one person who knew that Dana was right. One person who had witnessed Mark and Maralyn together.

She saw them one morning in the pool when *Merrem* was at her meeting. She'd heard them splashing and laughing in the pool. Maralyn was swimming without the top of her bikini. Mark had taken it off and thrown it into a tree.

She heard them in the study when *Merrem* was at the dentist. The door was locked. She heard them talking softly. She'd heard other sounds. Love-making sounds.

Then she heard Maralyn say, 'Mark! Give them back to me!'

She heard him say, 'No! I'm going to keep them in my pocket. I want to have them on me. To remind me of you…'

And Maralyn shriek with laughter and say, 'Don't be an idiot! Give my panties back to me…'

Minnie saw and heard these things. She knew what they were up to. Those two *skelms*…

She understood what Dana was feeling.

She recognised her despair and helplessness in knowing that her perceptions were being questioned, that others did not understand her terrible pain, that the betrayal of her husband and her friend was destroying the very core of her being.

She knew that feeling of being trapped. Of wanting to escape, to bring it all to an end. She knew that urge, that overwhelming all-encompassing urge to end it.

It had happened to her.

Silently, she stirred the prunes into the steaming pot of rich brown stew. Her face was like carved stone.

Again Dana's mother tried to speak to her. She tried to say that perhaps it wasn't as serious as Dana had made out. It looked worse than it was. She told her that Dana knew that Mark had always been a little bit of a flirt, like his dad and that a lot of men were like that. Most men, in fact. A pretty face…that's how men are…

She told Dana that Maralyn was who she was. She was always swaying around showing herself off. She was like that when she was a child of twelve. Didn't Dana remember how she was at twelve? Far beyond her years… Dana's mother thought that she would land up in real trouble, the way she was. She was only lucky she found a good guy to marry. Otherwise, who knows how things would have turned out for her?

But, said Dana's mother, twisting her rings, she was always a good friend to Dana. They'd gone through so much together. Their schooling, 'varsity, the weddings, the babies. They were like sisters. Although they were so different, Dana should not give up on Maralyn because Maralyn was basically a good friend and very loyal in her own way.

Dana's mother tried. Phone her, she said. Have it out with her. Clear the air. It's always good to clear the air. Get it off your chest. Come clean with how you feel. Give her a chance. She didn't mean to hurt you. I'm sure of that…

Dana said for God's sake what was she talking about? Didn't she understand? Mark was fucking her! Her husband and her best friend! This wasn't a flirtation. This wasn't a game. This was serious stuff! They were fucking!

'Oh, Dana please,' begged her mother.

'Don't Dana please me!' shouted the daughter. 'I know what I saw!'

'But,' said the mother, 'did you actually see them? Did you catch them in the act? That's what Dad says. He thinks that maybe you're over-reacting. You never actually caught them doing it…'

'Dad says… You say…' Dana's face was drained of colour, her thumbs clutched in her palms, her shoulders tense. She walked to the window, stared out, saw nothing and turned back to face her mother. 'Get out!' she shouted. 'You don't believe me. You're taking his side. You're taking her side. You're making me out to be a liar. Maybe you think I'm crazy! Mark thinks I'm crazy! I suppose you all think I'm crazy! Get out,' she screamed. 'Do me a favour! Just get out!'

The mother said OK OK she was going, but please, do one favour, phone Maralyn. At least do that…

She did phone Maralyn. Maralyn was not defensive. She listened and was measured in her answers. She did not deny sleeping with Mark but did not admit to it. She spoke of having a run with him, a swim with him. She said that Dana had been free to join them and why didn't she instead of sitting there sulking. She said that yes they were dancing closely, but they had both had too much to drink and that really, what's the big deal? She honestly believed that Dana had made a mountain out of a molehill, but, to be honest, she, Maralyn, did not want to be dragged down by all this. She had better things to do.

She ended the conversation by saying that perhaps they shouldn't be in contact for a while, have a break from each other. Let the dust settle.

On a grey day with the distant rumble of thunder and rain in the air, the two women were in the kitchen.

Minnie chopped carrots, celery, onions. Her nostrils burned, her eyes ran. She rubbed them with the backs of her arms.

From a large pot, mist rose and there was a smell of boiling meat bones. She removed the lid and skimmed the scum from the stock.

Outside, the wind whined and whipped the last leaves of summer. They carpeted the lawns and thickly covered the paths. They were crisp and brown, dancing madly in the wind.

Dana sat at the table, her hands cupping a mug of coffee. It had cooled and a skin covered the surface.

She'll ask Minnie to throw it out. She'll want a fresh one. A fresh coffee. Hot. With lots of boiled milk. This, too, she won't drink.

She glanced at the maid, at her broad back, the pink check of her uniform, the tied bow of her apron. She heard the knife chipping away at the carrots and celery.

'What are you making?' she asked. Her hair was lank and unwashed. It was eleven o'clock. She was in her dressing gown. Her feet were bare.

'Soup, *Merrem*.'

'Soup?'

'Vegetable soup.' The maid talked to the chopping board.

'*Merrem*? Granny phoned. She said I mus' remind you to take the long pink pill… Granny says please you musn' forget…'

In the distance there was the sound of thunder.

She glanced through the window and told herself to bring in the washing.

'Did *Merrem* remember? *Merrem*? To take the pink pill?'

'I think so. I don't know… I'm not sure…' Dana sighed. She passed her hand across her forehead.

'Would *Merrem* like some toas'? With egg?'

Dana shook her head. She listened to the vegetables plop into the pot.

Minnie turned round. Awkwardly. '*Merrem*? I'm going to eat my breakfast now. *Merrem*?' She cut two thick slices of bread and spread them with butter and jam. Hesitating, she took her mug and sandwiches and walked towards the back door.

She was not used to Madam sitting in the kitchen. She used to passed through, fly by, bag over shoulder, giving instructions. Now she was different. Not washing. Not dressing. Staying in her room. Sleeping. She was sitting at the kitchen table. She'd never sat at this table before.

Her presence made Minnie uneasy. She would eat her breakfast in her room.

'Oh, Minnie,' Dana said quickly. 'Can you have it here? Eat here? Please? I don't want to be on my own. Please sit here, at the table, and eat. That's if you don't mind…' Her eyes were glistening. Her heart beat fast and a pulse thumped in the side of her head. She could feel it with her hand. She shivered but her face felt flushed.

Minnie paused. Stared at her. Studied her. 'Are you sure, *Merrem*?'

'Yes, I'm sure. Please sit and be with me. I really don't want to be alone in the house.'

'OK, *Merrem*.' The maid sat tentatively, uncomfortably, holding onto the handle of her mug, her gaze fixed on the table.

There was silence. Minnie could not bring herself to eat the bread. She shifted her chair back a little and rubbed her knee with her hand.

'Tell me, Minnie, have you ever been married?' Dana's hands curled around the tops of her thin arms. With haunted eyes, she looked into Minnie's face, her swarthy skin, the pinpoints of tiny black moles, the scrubbed plainness of the woman, as though she were seeing her for the first time.

'I am married, *Merrem*.'

'You are? I've never seen your husband.'

Minnie felt Dana's eyes focus on her. She was silent, not knowing how to reply. She'd made a mistake, she thought. A bad mistake. She should not have said that. She should not have spoken about her husband. She thought she'd been tricked. She knew that Madam did not want men on the premises. She'd told her that many times. Even if she said the truth. Even if she tol' that they were separate. That she never seen him. Didn' seen him for years. Would the *Merrem* believe?

'I went away from him a long time ago.'

'So you're divorced?'

'No, *Merrem*. We never divorce. But we don' see each other. Never do we see…'

'Do you have children together?'

'No. No children. He have children. His firs' wife die. I help him with the children. But we have no kids.'

'And you? Do you have children?'

'No. No kids.'

'Could you not fall pregnant?'

A shadow moved darkly across Minnie's face. 'When I was very young, I fall.' Her voice faltered but she continued. 'My ma said I mus' have an abortion… It was a boy… But then I never fall pregnant after that.'

They were silent. The only sound was from the soup.

Dana said in a quiet voice, 'I also had an abortion. A couple of months after we came back from Plett. No one knows except my mother. Not even Master.'

'Same with me. Only my ma. Not my pa. No one else.'

'It was terrible.' Dana's eyes filled with tears.

'For me also.'

'It was also a boy. Another boy.'

Minnie waited. She was unsure where this talk would lead. She'd pushed the loss of her tiny boy into the furthest recesses of her mind. To be talking of it now seemed as though she was talking about someone else's abortion, someone else's baby.

Dana turned her wedding band around. She spoke softly, to herself.

'I couldn't have his child. Not after what went on in Plett. That was the last thing I needed. Another child by him… I wouldn't have wanted his child. Not his child. Not him. I want nothing do with him.'

She looked at Minnie, stared intently into her eyes. 'I want a divorce.' She sighed. Held her forehead. 'I can't do anything now. The doctor's advised me not to do anything at the moment. He said I must wait. He says I'm not strong enough.'

They sat together. Two women. Across the kitchen table.

Outside, the onslaught of a storm.

'She's not the first one, you know.' Dana's hands twisted together. 'He's had others… He's always been a flirt. Always eyeing someone. Wherever we went, he'd find someone to eye, someone to put his arm around. I've never caught him. He's very cunning. But I'm sure there were others. She wasn't the first one. And she won't be the last.'

Minnie saw Dana without looking at her. Saw her instinctively, the pain in her dark eyes, the slump of her thin shoulders, the nervous turning of her wedding ring.

Then, 'Why did you leave your husband?'

It was Minnie's turn to remember. Her turn to recall her pain. To recall what she had so resolutely attempted to eradicate from her mind. She'd never told anyone why she left. She'd remained stubbornly silent. There was no point in telling it. Her father would have thought she probably deserved it. Her mother might have cared but would have said nothing.

'He hit me. Very bad.'

'Why? Why did he do that?'

'I don' know. I try to be a good wife. I try to look after his kids. I cook. I clean. I do the washing. I also work to have my own money. I never take his money for me. On'y for the food. For the things in the house. But he hit me very bad. In my head. In my body. He punch me and he kick me. Then he say he's sorry. He won' do it again. Never again. But it's on'y for a time. Then it happen again… Very bad… He break my teeth. I stay in the house for two weeks before I can go out.

My face was big and there was blood come from my nose and black bruise in my eyes.'

Dana looked into the maid's flat eyes. 'That's terrible,' she whispered. 'So you left him?'

'*Ja.* I leave. I wait when he was at work. I pack my things. Then I leave. I never seen him again. It's a long time. Maybe five years.'

'Do you think you did the right thing? To leave him?'

'I mus' leave him. It was too hard. There was too much pain. Too much punishment for nothing. Can' do that any more. When I leave, I know that's the last time he hit me. And I say that's the las' time a man hit me… For what I mus' go through that? For what I did? Nothing!' Minnie wiped her eyes.

She had never expressed her feelings in this way before. Never cried… This was the first time…

Dana started to reach out to her, touched her hand.

The maid wiped her tears, sighed with her shoulders, and said, 'Yes. It is better. I'm by my own. But I'm safe. I'm still in my heart. It's quiet for me. Quiet in my life.'

Dana listened to her words, the words of this large and brooding woman. She heard her own hurt, her own suffering, in the words of this woman whose pain reflected her own.

She recalled the barrage of abuse from Mark the evening before. The banging of doors. The swearing. The four-letter words. Her face was not marked, but she was bruised and bleeding in her soul.

'I can't leave,' she said aloud to herself. 'Not now. Not with the kids.' But that is what she wanted. To leave. To pack a bag and go away. Like Minnie did. Get away from this terrible life. Away from this house. Away from the all the people that she thought crowded her. Closed her in.

I want a small room.

A secret room in a hidden place… Like her…

Two wounded women face to face across a table.

'Would *Merrem* like some soup? It can be nearly ready.'

'No, thanks. I couldn't eat a thing…' Listlessly, Dana lifted her hair from her neck, pushed it behind her ears. Her eyes welled with tears that fell and stained her dressing gown. 'I'm so tired,' she whispered. 'So tired.'

'Does *Merrem* want to rest? To lie in the bed? I can make the bed with clean sheets…'

Dana was still. She seemed far away. Then she said, 'Yes. Maybe I will.' She pushed herself away from the table. The bones of her shoulders were sharp and angled.

At the door, she turned to face the maid. 'Thank you, Minnie. Thanks for staying with me.'

In Dana's heart the marriage was over. The man she'd dedicated her life to, in her mind, was gone.

He came into the house, the man their children called Dad. He folded his tie in the same way, threaded his belt, fastened his shoelaces. His aftershave lingered, his hair was in the basin. There was his rumpled underwear, yesterday's socks.

It was all there but he was gone.

She knew what she'd seen. She knew they'd been intimate, although everyone was saying that she never actually caught them in the act. She'd accused him. She shouted. She screamed. She cried. She wrung her hands.

He watched her, his eyes like pinpricks, his mouth a thin line. He told her that she was a raving lunatic, that she was unbalanced, that she had a crazy overactive imagination.

He said that with all her antics, her hysterics, he could no longer trust her with the children. He told her that she was no longer competent. Was irrational. Unreliable. He turned the tables, neatly, deliberately, and left her in a heightened state of extreme anxiety and stress.

She should have known that Mark could not be challenged. He was a vicious opponent. No one knew better than him how to fight, how to use words to destroy, how to play on other people's emotions, how to manipulate situations to his advantage.

Dana was no match for him. She struggled to keep a balance between her resolve to leave him and his threats about her competency as a mother. She knew that he could take the children from her if she left.

She had been betrayed.

At times, her heart was heavy and swollen. She felt it burst with anguish. At other times, she felt dry and hollow and inconsequential. She thought that she might blow away.

Her mother said to give it time. Time is a great healer.

Her psychologist listened, heard her desperation and her intense desire to escape from the marriage. He understood the dire consequences of that divorce. He had no answer for her. He suggested a marriage counsellor. She did not want that.

She did not want Mark.

Dana blundered about in a dark fog of confusion and anguish.

She moved into the spare bedroom that seemed foreign, and, like her, not part of the house. It was the only room without a view, facing an angle of the roof where the tiles looked compressed and uncomfortable.

She lay for hours on the unfamiliar bed staring, unseeing, at the blank white wall.

Her psychologist suggested that she see a friend of his, a psychiatrist who could prescribe something, some medication, to help her.

She refused.


She wanders around the house. Tentatively, she stands at the doors of her sons' rooms. She straightens a bed cover, opens a cupboard door. The shirts and shorts are neatly stacked. Minnie, she thinks. The boys aren't like this. They're messy.

She goes into her bedroom. The bed looks huge. Shots of silk in the bedspread catch light. She stares at her side of the bed. She can't recall sleeping there.

She touches the stoppers of perfume bottles on the dressing table, looks vacantly at the blue contents of one, the gold of another. She does not see them as hers, does not open them to smell their perfumes, does not dab a little on her wrist.

Mark's shoes lie next to his side of the bed. Minnie knows to leave them there. Dana sees them, sees his wristwatch, some small change, a magazine on cars.

She opens her cupboard and stares at her clothes. The slacks, the shirts, the skirts, all are immaculately hanging, the scarves are in their individual bags, her handbags in their plastic coverings, her shoes in pairs on the rack.

Downstairs, she moves quietly through the lounge, her thin frame outlined against the light. The sun catches a glow in her hair that is tied back and clean, recently washed by her mother.

Through the open doors there is a dappled pattern of leaves. The tiles on the patio warm her feet. Wearily, she sits on a chair of wrought iron, sinks back against its white cushions.

A gentle movement of air brushes across her face. The sun is there also, to comfort her.

Leaves in the plane tree rustle. There is the buzz of a bee, the subtle scents of roses, fragrances that for a moment she knows.

A flock of birds are small dots in the sky.

There is a whisper of cloud, a translucent crescent of moon.

She does not think why that sliver of moon should be there at this time of day. She does not think of anything.

She closes her eyes. There is too much light. Too much happening.

She wants to go back to her room.

She wants to sleep.

The garden was green and still after the rain. A distant cloud hung, unsure, in the sky, lightly changing shape. The trees sparkled and bubbles of rain clung to petals. From freesias and roses, sweet perfumes fused and flowed.

A bee buzzed. There was the chirrup of a bird. A car drove past the house.

Minnie, usually filled with purpose, stood hesitating on the path fingering the secateurs. The rose garden was the domain of her Madam.

But Dana had not been there for a while. The blooms were neglected. Overblown. Their petals scattered.

Minnie thought to cut a few, jus' one or two. For Dana.

She thought of Dana – how pale she looked, her head on the pillow, her dank hair falling across her face. She thought of her listless hands, those hands that would cut roses, strip the thorns from their stems, and arrange them in tall vases, in round vases, in a cut-glass crystal bowl that reflected a thousand tiny rainbows. Roses that filled the rooms with essence and beauty.

She thought that she would cut a few roses, put them in a vase and take them to the spare room. She could put them on the little side table. She would go in quietly, not wake *Merrem*, and put the flowers there. Next to her bed. So when she wake, she will see them. Smell them. Then maybe they make her feel better. She loves the flowers. She always look soft when she work with the flowers. Maybe if I do this, it make her feel better.

That is what Minnie thought standing on the path.

She cut three white roses, held them gingerly, and placed them in a vase that Madam never used, a vase that had stood at the back of a cupboard, a white clay vase with a small spray of violets painted across it.

Quietly, she opened the door. Madam was asleep, her arm across her face.

Minnie placed the vase gently on the table, adjusted one of the blooms, looked at the arrangement, then looked at Dana.

'*Haai,*' she whispered.

Her face creased with concern. She held her hands. She shook her head. Then silently she slipped out of the room.

Dana's father found the steps difficult. He pulled on the bannister and dragged one foot. She was sitting at the window. The curtain was drawn and the room looked grey.

'Hi,' he said. 'Do you mind if I come in?'

Her dull gaze slid towards the door. He had not seen her for a few days. Her eyes had sunk into her waxen face. Her cheekbones, her nose and her chin were more prominent, and her hair hung lank and limp.

His heart sank. This girl is ill, flashed through his mind. Really ill. 'Dana.' He sat heavily on the unmade bed. 'Hi.'

'Hello.' She stared at her hands.

'How're you doing?'

'As you see…'

'Thought I'd pop by. See how you are. Ma and I've been thinking about you a lot. You know. You and Mark. We think about all of you all the time. Also the kids…'

'I know.' She turned to him, her eyes dark and frightened. Her voice was desperate. 'I'm trapped, Dad. I can't stay here and I can't leave without the kids… He threatens to take them from me and he'll do it, he'll take the kids… He says I'm not fit to be their mother…'

'Well, he can't just do that.' Her father lifted his gaze. 'He may think he can, but I can tell you he can't.' He looked at her with purpose. 'He hasn't come across me yet… You may be a soft target, but I'm a different kettle of fish.'

'You won't be able to do anything. If we get divorced, the courts will only look at him and me. I won't stand a chance against him…'

'Well, that's why I've come to see you. I've given this a lot of thought. I've fought many battles in my life and I've seen a lot and

I've learned a lot.' He leaned forward, his brow furrowed, his old eyes sharply focussed. 'Dana, let me speak plain. Let me tell you the way you're carrying on, you're right. You don't stand a snowball's chance. That's why I'm here. That's why I've come. To tell you why you're not gonna win this…'

'How will that help? I don't need you to tell me that…' Her voice sharpened. She turned away.

Knowing that he could be dismissed, be told to go, he quickly intervened. He did not want to lose the opportunity to tell her what he had mulled over for days. 'Dana,' he said with urgency, 'you're losing out because you're playing right into his hands. You're doing exactly what he wants you to do. You're the person he cheated on, but he's not going there. Instead, he's telling you that you're crazy…'

'So why…'

He held up his hands. She stared at them. Big blunt hands, freckled and bulging with blue veins. Old hands that begged her to listen. 'What you've got to do is play him at his own game. He thinks he's big and powerful, that he wields the bat. You've allowed that…'

'Dad, please…'

'Just listen to me. For a minute. Please. Look at you. Look what you've allowed him to do. You've locked yourself in this little room when half the house belongs to you. You're a half-owner. But you put yourself in this little room. Why are you sleeping here? Tell me that. Why aren't you sleeping in your bedroom? In the bed we gave you as a wedding present. I saw when I came up that he's taken over the whole bed. With books and papers on your side. Why are you allowing that? It's your bed.

'And this house… You've got to reclaim this house. It's your house, your home. You decorated it. You looked after it like gold. It's all your doing. And remember, you own half of it. Half of it is yours…

'And your kids? He's running around with them. His parents are running around with them. We're running around with them and you, by locking yourself away, you're handing them over on a plate. Reclaim them. For God's sake. They're your kids. You gave birth to them. You brought them up. You watched over them like no other mother I know. Now look what you've done. You've virtually given them up…

'And one other thing I need to say, and I need to say this because you're my child, my little girl, and because I love you more than anything in the world…' Tears leaked into the lines of his face.

'Dana, look at yourself. Look how you look. Listen to me. You're a beautiful girl. You were given a gift. Beauty is a gift. It's not for everyone. But you have it. You were given it. Natural beauty. Don't destroy such a wonderful precious gift. Reclaim it, my darling. Reclaim your beauty… Come out of this little room. Come back into the light. Take what is rightfully yours…'

'Dad…'

'Listen to me. Listen to what I'm telling you. Don't fight him any more. If he's rude, ignore him. If he insults you, pretend not to hear him. The stronger you are, the less he'll be able to pull you down. Don't give him so much importance. At all times, act like a lady. Be polite. But, most important, reclaim what is yours. Reclaim your life. For yourself and your children. In your home. You owe this to yourself. Try it. That's all I ask. See if it works. I'll help you. I'll be there for you every step of the way.

'To tell the truth, I don't know how the big picture will play out. But one thing I do know. If you don't come back at him in a different way, in a clever way, you're going to go one way and that's down. You're gonna lose wholesale. I don't want to see that. I don't want to see you lose. You're not a loser. You never have been. You're a clever girl. Now's the time to prove to yourself what you're made of.'

He gently took her hand in his, her thin long-fingered hand in his big square one, and said in a gruff and muffled voice, 'Dana, do it for yourself, my darling. Do it for you.'

It was a slow process. Timorous. Tentative. Like something newborn. Dana had to find strength in her legs, flexibility in her hands. She had to learn to hold her head up again. To look with her eyes and see. She had to hear. She had to learn to feel.

She spent her first few weeks walking tentatively around the house. Through the garden. Sitting at the pool.

On a hot day, she put her feet in the water, saw their image distorted by the ripples, and took them out quickly. But then she did it again and, gaining courage, took off her wrap and cautiously lowered herself into the pool. She was numb with shock as the cold water moved up her legs and reached her waist. She stood breathless and still. The sun beat down and egged her on.

'Go on,' it seemed to say. 'Go in. Cool off.'

She drew in a deep breath and ducked under the water. Gasping, she stood up holding onto the side. Then she bent her knees and slowly lowered herself again. She found herself striking out to the deep end and swimming back again.

The cold water, the movement of her arms and legs, awakened something in her, something good.

Without being reminded, she began to shower each day, and shampoo her hair, and brush her teeth. She tied her hair back and dressed in tracksuits, not wanting to wear her clothes or put on her rings. But that did not matter. What counted was that Dana was beginning to care for herself again.

In the afternoons, she sat in the lounge sipping tea. It was a room that harboured the sun. She gazed at the patterns in the lustrous wooden surfaces, the whorls of gold and red, the chocolate browns and the pale creams, flowing and harmonious, as though created by some existential artist.

She felt the rich tightly packed woollen coverings, ran her hands over the sensuous velvets, watched the rich interchange of colour in the Persian rugs. She'd never spent time on her own in this room. It was a space that had been created only for visitors.

Now she sat for long hours seeing and touching that which she had carefully composed. She heard the voices. The comments. The endless compliments.

So tasteful.

Such a good eye.

Put it together like nobody else can…

Ask Dana to come with you…

In her mind, she heard the comments. With those, came the memories.

The more she saw of the living rooms, the more she disliked what she saw.

She went to the backyard on a windy day when the sheets were blowing, recalling how she'd loved to run through the wash lines as a child, to hide there, to feel the damp clothes against her, to smell their fresh smell.

Dana stood there now. She breathed in the wind.

The dog came up to her, looked at her intently with soft eyes.

'Hello, Blackie,' she whispered, touching his ears. 'Hello, Blackie.'

In the long silence of the days and in the emptiness of the mornings, she was comforted by Minnie's quiet presence. There was the swish of a broom, the running of a tap, the sight of a duster moving in circles determinedly across a table.

There was a tray of tea, some hot toast, a comforting bowl of soup. It came quietly and unobtrusively. To wherever she was.

Dana's recovery had taken time.

One of her visitors was Jono. On a Saturday afternoon, he arrived unannounced at the house. Minnie opened the door and swiftly turned away, hoping that he would not recognise her.

Dana was delighted to see him. She cried and he held out his arms to her, not minding that her tears were soaking his black silk shirt.

They sat on the patio sipping lemonade. She told him all that had happened and he listened intently, his dark eyes compassionate.

'What a bitch!' he called Maralyn. 'What an absolute bitch!'

'It wasn't all her, ' protested Dana. 'Mark was just as guilty.'

'I don't think so.' Jono had firm ideas on how people functioned. 'It's always the women. They give the signals. They start the fires. The men just follow. And that one, I've seen how she puts out the scent. She's like a bitch on perpetual heat.'

He reached across the table and gently lifted her long dank hair. 'Sweetheart.' His voice was gentle. 'This needs some attention. It's a bit dry. A bit tired. If you like, I'll see to it for you. Would you like that?'

'Oh, Jono... It's Saturday afternoon. You've been working the whole week. I think it's wonderful of you to come, but not to work. I wouldn't expect that.'

'Angel. This isn't work. It's a pleasure. My favourite girl with such gorgeous hair. But it does need some attention. Some loving care.'

With the lightest touch, he shampooed her hair and massaged warm oil into her scalp.

Minnie brought tea and sandwiches. He glanced at her. For a moment thought that he knew her. Then he took out his scissors, the only pair he ever used. His magic scissors, he called them, rubbing their edges against a small knife sharpener.

'Dana,' he said kindly, 'darling, I think it would be a good idea to give your hair a really good cut. We need to take off quite a bit to give it back its strength again. What do you think?' He waited, apprehensive, knowing how vain Dana had always been about her hair, how she loved flicking it back, tucking it behind her ears.

She sat quietly fingering the long lifeless strands, then she turned to him and said, 'Do whatever you think, Jono. I really don't mind.'

'Are you sure?' he asked, suddenly anxious.

'Yes. I'm sure. Perhaps the best is to cut it short.'

'OK. Let's do it. A lovely chic short bob. It'll look wonderful. Show off your lovely face. And you can always grow it. That's the beauty about hair. It always grows back.'

Dana never grew her hair again. Her hairstyle became part of her new image. She was still beautiful but in a retiring and unobtrusive way. She wore little make-up and no jewellery. Her clothes were loose-fitting, almost baggy. She favoured unconstructed linen or woollen jackets that hung well on her thin frame.

Some of her friends remained although she seemed to have little to say to them. They stayed in touch anyway, dropping by, or taking her for coffee, or going for a walk along the sea. They felt her slip away, but they kept in touch, irrespective. In one way or another.

Dana was grateful. Although she found it difficult to talk to them, she appreciated their concern. It was good to know that they cared.

She took up art.

The studio was in Kalk Bay, a suburb where Whites and Coloureds lived side by side, somehow tolerated by the authorities.

It was a fishing village, its residents closely connected to the sea. To boats. To nets. To catches. Its small harbour was a hive of activity. From here, the fishermen sailed each day before sunrise. Fish were brought back, great hauls of stock fish, yellow tail, *kabeljou, snoek*, to this busy trading place where shop owners and restauranteurs and housewives came to feel, to choose, to buy.

Where loud voices bargained. Prices were argued. Deals were done.

Where women, enveloped in yellow oilskin aprons, *doeks* on their heads, their haunches on low stools, gossiped and laughed showing gaps between teeth, complained, swore, and cleaned the fish.

The skilled flash of their sharp knives scraped the skins, showering everything with silver scales, sliced along the lengths of fish, expertly removed the bones.

They were surrounded by fish heads in buckets. Oysters. Clams. Crabs. Crayfish in the colours of fire groping in tin baths.

Dana would come early, sit on the sea wall and watch.

The fishermen.

The scuffed boats bobbing in their moorings.

The clusters of women.

The customers, the sounds of their loud voices.

The cry of seagulls vociferously demanding their share of the booty.

The smell of the fish.

The quay…

And beyond that the sea from Muizenberg to Simonstown to the hazy outline of Gordon's Bay.

Dana needed a blank canvas for her art and also for her life. She needed light and space. She wanted no separation from the sun and moon and stars, from the air, the clouds, the sky. From day and night.

The window coverings came down. The velvets, the voiles, the heavily lined silks. Light blinds replaced them. The windows now opened the house to the garden, and, depending on the position of the sun, either reflected trees and clouds in their panes, or gave the impression that there was nothing between the rooms and the outside.

She sold the antiques and replaced damask and velvet with sleek leather couches. A large oak coffee table was the only table in the lounge. All the little side tables, exquisitely crafted with marquetry, went. The armoire, the credenza, the bureaus, a *cabriole*, a chaise longue, the console, the vitrine, all the gilding and all the gilt, were sold at an auction to which she did not bother to go.

She did keep the silk Qum Persian carpet. It was the first item she and Mark had bought. At first she'd hesitated, not wanting any recollections of him in the house. But the colours were entrancing. The reds. The blues. The composition of its images – squares of woven flowers, small golden candelabras – juxtapositioned. This giant woven pure silk patchwork had always captivated and enthralled her. Yes. She decided she would keep the rug.

The huge crystal chandeliers, lanterns and lamps were replaced by tiny lights that shone like stars in the ceilings. A glass dining table and light Swedish chairs replaced the huge antique dining suite.

The only ornaments were what she could find in her garden. There were bowls of lemons or plums. Roses, plum-coloured proteas and thorny orange stems of berries. Stems of leaves and stems that were brown and brittle. In winter, a small vase of snowdrops, in summer a bowl of sweet smelling freesias, ranunculas and anemones. Always, vases of roses.

She had the walls painted white and mostly they were blank. In the lounge was one of her paintings, and one other in the dining room. She favoured shades of blue, but there touches of white and cream, and an occasional burst of burning yellow. Brooding scenes, but quiet and soothing.

She met a man in her sculpture class, a retired medical specialist. He'd told her that during the past few years he'd rejected his strict Catholic upbringing – the dogmas imposed on him in his youth. Now, in his latter life, he'd, in his own words, become free-thinking and emancipated.

They spent time together, walked in the vineyards, drank wine, watched the waves. They climbed the mountain, took drives into the country, saw the opera. They shared picnics in the forest and swam in the sea. They ate in little restaurants and sat talking over coffee and warm scones.

They held hands.

He'd wanted more from her, wanted her to love him, but there was a part of her, deep within her, that did not recover, that would not recover, that remained as cold and contained as the mountain.

She sipped her tea.

She saw the plane trees, the lawns, the rose garden. They seemed to have lost their lustre. Became faded. Jaded.

When the boys leave, she told herself, I'll sell the house. It'll be time to move on.

I'll find a nice apartment. Something with a sea view.

And a decent room for Minnie…

I t was Sue-Ellen on the phone, hysterical. '*Hulle is dood geskiet!*'
'*Wie? Wat praat jy?*'

'*Die* police! They shot them dead. *Drie seuns!*' She was shouting and crying and did not make sense.

To make matters more difficult, Jackson was making a deafening noise with the lawn mower and Minnie, who had never sat on the chair next to the hall table, did so now and covered one ear with a cupped hand.

She pieced together what had happened.

At Alexander Sinton School, in Athlone, and around that area, several anti-apartheid protests, particularly involving students, had taken place. Security police were sent to crush a gathering of young people protesting against the government.

A South African railways truck had been loaded with crates. The truck looked innocuous but, in fact, was harbouring armed police hidden among the crates. The truck drove down Thornton Street into the centre of the protest. Police on the truck began firing. Three boys were killed.

'From our people. The Coloureds. Three boys from our people.' Sue-Ellen was shaking, screaming. 'And lots injured. Lots more injured. They hid in the truck! *Die fokken* police! Hiding like cowards! Those pigs! The swines! They shot our boys. Because of apartheid! Because of the laws they make against our people. Because we stand for our rights! Because we also human! They kill us! They shoot us! They kill our boys!'

Jackson had become sullen. The week before, he threw the lunch Minnie had given him into the bin, making sure that she saw him do it.

'*Haai* Jackson. *Wat doen jy? Jy's onbeskof!* What are you doing? Throwing the food…'

'I don't eat this. Every week the Saldanha pilchards. For all the time I'm here. All these years, this rubbish food. Not even for a dog…' His face was dark, his eyes flat.

She tried to disguise the pilchards, mashed them and made rissoles. She added sliced tomato and buttered bread.

He took the plate without looking at her.

Mid-afternoon she saw him sitting under the plane tree at the pool, his tools scattered. *Merrem* had told him to mow the lawn, to skim the pool.

'*Haai* Jackson. *Wat makeer? Is jy siek?*'

'Yes. I'm sick. Here. In my heart.'

'Why?'

'My son's not in the school. The school's burnt. He's running with his friends. He's not learning. He only wants to burn things. With his friends. To break things. To throw stones. It's very dangerous what he does. He can die. He can be kill.'

'You mus' tell him not to do these things…'

'To tell him. He won' listen to me. The kids don' listen. They got fathers. They got mothers, but they in charge of us! They angry. They full with hate. They say this is a bad country. A bad government. He tell me the Tricameral party they now make in the parliament is for Coloureds, for Indians, for Whites. Not for Blacks. We got no say. He tell me that. We got no voice. We got no representation. We mus' vote in the Homelands. They say South Africa is not our home. Only the Homelands is our home. They fill with angry. So they take this now by themselves in their hands. In the locations, they make the fires, burn the shacks, burn the tyres. They run in their school uniforms. They kids. There are police, the soldiers. They got guns. They shoot. My son can die…'

He looked at her, looked into her eyes. 'Things are very bad,' he said. 'Very bad. But it will not stop. They can have the police. They can call the army. But it will not stop. This is going to get more big. This fight will get more…'

He paused, weighing his words. 'It is all for the Whites, this country. The Blacks got nothing. There is too much hate for the Whites. But they will get it also. For sure. All these people…' His outstretched arm indicated the people who lived in the houses, those who lived in the street. 'They can get kill too…'

'But you would not do anything to the *Merrem*? You been working here a long time. You wouldn' do anything to them?'

He squinted into the sun. 'Me?' His reply was slow, measured. 'No. Not me… But…' His grin was ugly, his eyes veiled. 'The gardener down the road. He don' care. He don' know this people where we work. He only know they White. If he want, he can kill them. He don' know them. He don' care…'

'Jeez! We're in big shit you know! God knows how we'll ever get this right! All these riots and demonstrations… All this shooting and killing…'

'And what about the fucking boycotts and stay-aways! What chance does the economy have with all this shit going on every day…'

'And the whole world against us…'

'What about our safety? What about our kids? We're next. They'll come after us. For sure.'

'We should get the bladdy hell outa here!'

'This place is finished. *Kaput!* No chance! A fucked-up bladdy country!'

Every now and then, Dana found herself reflecting on the years that she and Mark shared.

She allowed herself to go back to their first year together, and how much they'd thought that they loved each other.

She reflected on the fragility of love and how easily it is destroyed... How quickly love turns to hate...

She recalled that the break-up, considering the storms that had gone before, had, thankfully, been fairly amicable.

Without argument, Mark had given her the house. He'd also agreed that Jeremy and Jarryd live with her. Perhaps because, in his clinical way, he'd already moved on.

Within a few years, he married a much younger woman, one of his secretaries, with whom he had a daughter. They chose to live on the other side of the mountain and made new friends.

But she did see him occasionally.

One evening, he was sitting a few rows in front of her at the theatre, and she noted that he was now quite grey.

The boys remained in constant contact with their father and he took great interest in their progress, their education and their social life. He wanted to know the marks they got, whether they needed extra lessons, whether they were on track for getting into their chosen professions at university. He kept abreast of their girlfriends and the friends they kept and wanted to know that they were behaving themselves. He took them on holidays, spent time with them, bought their clothes, presented them with cars.

Jeremy was in his final year of accountancy, Jarryd in second year law. As Dana's father said, they were good boys.

Despite everything, the parents had a done a good job. They were boys you could be proud of. Lovely boys.

But, they'd told Dana, they would leave. Once they'd finished their degrees, they would leave South Africa. There was no way they'd go into the army, which they would be compelled to do. They would not go into the locations with guns and shoot the blacks. They were not part of this war. In fact, they couldn't wait to get out. They would leave. Go to Australia or America.

Dana accepted their decisions calmly. It was the way of many young men. They left South Africa. Washed their hands of the mess, the chaos, insurmountable problems that their country faced.

Hopefully, when the time came for her sons, they'd choose to go to the same place… Her boys… These brothers… Hopefully be near each other. And always be there for each other.


It was at Jarryd's wedding that Minnie got to wear her pink dress. His bride had chosen pink for her theme, for her retinue, for all the flowers at the reception.

'Pink!' Dana groaned. 'I hate pink. It's my worst colour. I look terrible in pink.'

She would have to tone in, they told her. She mustn't start out on the wrong foot. Not with the new daughter-in-law. It'll only be for one day. She need never wear the outfit again.

They said it didn't have to be pink-pink. It could be dusty pink, or rose pink, or a mauve pink, or beige with a pink tint, or pink with a beige tint.

As long as she toned in…

Minnie took her dress from its plastic covering with trembling hands. It still had the label on it. The price! She could not believe that she'd paid such a price for it. A Stuttafords price…

She waited for Dana to go out so that she could try it on in front of the full-length mirror.

She took off her uniform and slipped into the dress. It fitted perfectly.

She pushed her feet into the silver sandals and clipped the pearl necklace around her neck.

She looked at herself in the mirror twenty years after last seeing herself in the dress.

She stared at her reflection, at her dark face sprinkled with minute black moles, at her broad nose, at her grey hair held by pins in a tight bun. She remembered her haircut and the blue rinse Jono had given her.

She looked at her figure, at her square body, her heavy legs.

But what she saw was a beautiful pink satin dress that fell in the softest of shiny folds, a gleaming dress with a sweetheart neckline complemented by silver sandals and a pink pearl that lay in the crease between her breasts.

She picked up the silver clutch bag and held it as she'd seen *Merrem* hold hers. In her hand with her arm held straight down, close to her side, against her skirt.

She turned slowly in front of the mirror, first this way, then that. She took a few steps forward, then back again.

She stood quite still for a few moments watching herself. A happy feeling welled up in her.

She fronted the mirror again and thought that she looked nice.

Reelly nice.

Smart.

Jus' like her *Merrem*.

* 9 7 8 1 7 6 0 4 1 6 1 3 3 *